CHANGE FOR THE WORSE

CHANGE FOR THE WORSE

by

Elizabeth Lemarchand

Dales Large Print Books
Long Preston, North Yorkshire,
BD23 4ND, England.

British Library Cataloguing in Publication Data.

Lemarchand, Elizabeth
    Change for the worse.

    A catalogue record of this book is
    available from the British Library

    ISBN   978-1-84262-583-5 pbk

First published in 1981

Published in Large Print 2009 by arrangement with
Elizabeth Lemarchand, care of Watson, Little Ltd.

Dales Large Print is an imprint of Library Magna Books Ltd.

Printed and bound in Great Britain by
T.J. (International) Ltd., Cornwall, PL28 8RW

TO
CICELY CHICHESTER

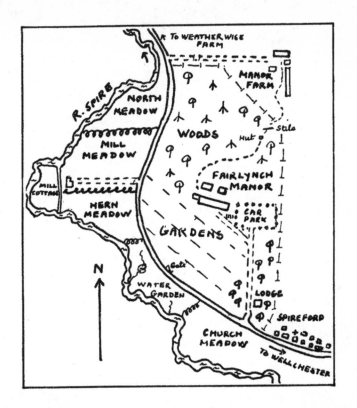

WYNSHIRE

FAIRLYNCH MANOR, Spireford. 6 miles NW of Wellchester; turn right on Wellchester–Midbury road.

Attractive Regency house (opening 1978). Woods, terraced gardens and a water garden. Open daily from first Saturday in April to last in September 2– 5.30 pm. Dogs must be left in car park. Admission: 60p. Children and Pensioners 30p. Pre-arranged parties at 20 per cent reduction: apply to the Warden (tel: Spireford 333).

From: *Heritage of Britain Properties*, 1977.

Chief Characters

Katharine Ridley, widow, formerly of
  Fairlynch Manor
Alexandra Parr (Alix), her granddaughter
Francis Peck, Warden of Fairlynch Manor
Hilary Peck, his wife
Christopher Peck, his son
Hugo Rossiter RA, of Mill Cottage,
  Spireford
Malcolm and Lydia Gilmore, a business
  couple of Weatherwise Farm, Spireford
Professor Digby Chilmark, MA, D.Litt., art
  adviser to Heritage of Britain
George Palmer, a visitor to Fairlynch
  Manor
David and Julian Strode, near neighbours of
  the Pollards
Detective Chief Superintendent Tom
  Pollard of New Scotland Yard
Detective-Inspector Gregory Toye, also of
  New Scotland Yard

Prologue

David and Julian Strode sat over aperitifs in the Piazza del Duomo at Portrova, writing picture postcards to their small son and daughter in London. On examining the contents of his wallet David announced that they only had one stamp left.

'I'll go and find a *tabacchi*,' he said, 'and have a look round for somewhere to eat. Why not stay here in the shade? I suppose it's too late to go and see the cathedral before the siesta shut-down?'

'I don't know that there's an awful lot to see,' Julian replied. 'I looked it up in the guide book last night, and it says the nave was largely rebuilt in the eighteenth century and is highly ornate, which sounds ominous. How about my nipping across now while you're getting stamps, and then we'll know if it's worth coming back later?'

'O.K.,' he agreed. 'We'll meet in the porch if you're thrown out at twelve.' He tipped the waiter and pocketed the rest of his change. 'My God, it's hot!'

He departed. The waiter replaced the chair which he had deftly whisked away, and bowed and smiled at the signora inglese.

'Very 'ot, signora,' he agreed. *'Molto caldo, oggi.'*

Julian's Italian was minimal. She smiled back at him as she collected her belongings and gestured in the direction of the cathedral.

'Il Duomo,' she ventured.

The waiter swelled visibly with local patriotism.

'Bellissimo, signora! Stupendo!'

She tied a silk scarf over her head and stepped out into the sun-baked piazza, a small slight figure with dark hair and expressive brown eyes. Heat rose up at her from the dusty ground. She walked slowly, revelling in high summer and the feeling of being on holiday. The Strodes had flown their car out to Milan and were heading in a leisurely way for Venice, stopping off to explore lesser-known places. Portrova had turned out to be an attractive small city as yet little spoilt by industrialization. The cathedral square was happily inaccessible to cars and a useful short cut for pedestrians. As she strolled across it Julian saw that there were no longer many people about, as though life were running down to its suspension in the siesta. There was a sudden metallic rattle and crash as a shop lowered its shutters prematurely. The windows of upper storeys were already shuttered, giving the houses a withdrawn, even secretive appearance. She stepped aside to avoid two children in black pinafores absorbed in hitting each other with their school satchels, and paused to study the Romanesque west front of the cathedral.

There was a fine rose window flanked by frescoes of haloed monastic figures, recently and not too skilfully restored. The porch was supported by slender pillars resting on the backs of marble lions, their aggressiveness subdued by the passage of centuries. Julian took off her sunglasses and went up a short flight of steps.

As she paused to let her eyes adjust to comparative darkness her spine prickled. An unmistakeably human bundle was lying on the ground, partly propped against the door. It moved slightly and she relaxed. She had not after all come upon a corpse, with all the attendant complications of doing so in a foreign country. She looked down on an old woman with a shrivelled face, thin wisps of white hair, and a pair of sharp black eyes which were fixed upon her with the unwinking stare of a bird. The bundle-like effect was produced by layers of shapeless garments, and the remains of a pair of dusty black shoes were bound on with strips of rag. Slowly a thin dirty hand emerged and was silently held out.

Discomfited by an immediate sense of guilt, Julian took a thousand lire note from her handbag. Fingers deformed by arthritis closed on it.

'*Che Dio La benedice, signora.*'

There was no beggar's whine in the voice, even a touch of dignity. Feeling at a loss Julian gave a little bow and turned to enter the cathedral, aware that she was under close scrutiny.

The interior was dark and felt chilly, and she threw a cardigan round her shoulders. An overpowering ornate high altar loomed in the distance behind a row of dim red lamps suspended from the roof, and there was a vast organ. Priests and worshippers were completely absent, and this contributed to the depressing atmosphere of the building. Remembering that she had very little time Julian walked up the south aisle, peering into one side-chapel after another but discovering nothing that seemed of much interest. She stopped at the entrance to the choir which

18

looked more promising, and glanced round in the hope of seeing a slot machine that would provide a short period of electric lighting in exchange for a hundred lire coin.

'*Si chiude! Si chiude!*'

An eerie sound suddenly echoed through the cathedral, swirling upwards to the roof. Startled, and for a moment completely baffled, Julian stood motionless. Then the slamming of a door down at the west end and the unmistakable turning of a key in a lock sent her running full tilt down the long nave.

'Wait! Wait!' she shouted urgently, groping for the Italian word. '*Turista inglese!*'

Her voice was abruptly drowned in the clamour of the cathedral clock striking the four quarters and the twelve strokes of the hour. It was obvious that nobody could possibly hear either her cries or her pounding on the inside of the door. She paused for breath and to let the noise subside, and in the same moment was aware of someone just behind her. Before she could swing round her cardigan was whipped over her head and a strong hand pressed over her mouth.

She struggled frantically as she was dragged away from the door, but realised that she had been attacked by two people. The sleeves of her cardigan were knotted at the back of her neck, her hands tied behind her with her scarf and her ankles secured. Then she was hoisted up and carried further into the cathedral. Sick with terror and convinced that she was being kidnapped, she pleaded with her captors, repeating 'Inglese, inglese', through the muffling folds of her cardigan. Their chilling silence heightened her panic. Her heart was pounding so violently that she felt it must soon burst. Her mind began to behave strangely, her normal life with David and the children receding from her like a picture being borne away. The only reality was here and now, with its incredibility and hideous possibilities.

She was unceremoniously dumped on a hard surface, and for a moment sensed a wordless exchange in progress. Then followed sounds of stealthy withdrawal. She lay faint with apprehension until a loud noise of wood being smashed and splintered roused her. She caught her breath and waited. The noise was repeated from a little further away, and still more remote sounds became audible which she could not interpret. Now, she thought, they'll come back and get me. Take me out by a side door somewhere to a car they've got waiting... Tears ran down her cheeks as she pictured David perhaps only a few yards away, wondering where she had gone...

No one came. Absolute silence had descended. For the first time Julian realised how acutely uncomfortable she was, and tried to shift her position. She was wearing sandals, and as she moved her toes encountered something smooth and yielding. She explored its surface gingerly, and to her amazement identified her handbag.

The physical contact with a familiar object acted on her incoherent thinking like a catalyst. They had not raped, abducted or even robbed her. And she was certain that somehow they had got out of the cathedral and gone... They must simply have wanted to prevent her from seeing what they were doing ... a robbery, from the sound of it...

There was sudden rattling and shouting at the west door. Although the chances of whoever was outside hearing her were negligible, she shouted as loudly as she could. The rattling stopped. It *must* be David, she told herself. Surely he'd somehow got an idea that she was inside, and now would get hold of somebody who understood English?

Unbelievably the chimes of the first quarter broke out overhead. Could it all really have happened in only quarter of an hour?

She waited tensely with her ears strained for the slightest sound, dealing resolutely with small recurring tremors of fear. There was an apparently timeless interval.

Suddenly a lot of things happened at once. A key grated in a lock, there were hurried footsteps and David's voice, sharp with anxiety, was calling her.

'Here! I'm here!' she called, heaving herself on to her side to attract his attention. As she bumped down a step he fielded her.

'*Mamma mia!*' bellowed a powerful Italian throat.

'And all the chaps nicked was the loose cash in the alms boxes they busted open?' Detective Chief Superintendent Tom Pollard asked, reclining at ease in one of the Strodes' armchairs, his hands clasped behind his head.

He and his wife Jane, near neighbours and close friends, had come round to drinks the evening after the Strodes' return from Italy.

'So the cathedral people said,' David Strode replied. 'The padre who produced the key told me that all the plate was kept in a safe in the sacristy. All the same, there was quite a lot of stuff around. Candlesticks, for instance, and a cross on the high altar with some valuable stones set in it. Easy enough to prise out, you'd think.'

'Given time,' Jane Pollard remarked. 'Obviously they'd banked on a couple of hours at least. It was Julian turning up that dished everything.'

'How did they get out?' Pollard asked.

'Through the small door at the east end. It had a mortice lock, but the sacristan johnny was in the habit of leaving the key in it during the siesta closing, apparently. I gathered that he was going to be for it in a big way.'

'I couldn't help being sorry for him,' Julian said. 'He looked like a hunted rabbit, and the priest was about six foot six and broad to match, and roared at him like a mad bull.'

'Sorry my foot,' David retorted, getting up to refill their glasses. 'He damn well deserved anything he got, the lazy little bastard. If he'd done his job properly you wouldn't have got shut in in the first place.'

'There's a bit of this enthralling story missing,' Jane pointed out. 'David, how did you know Julian was shut in, especially when she didn't answer when you banged on the door?'

'My old woman,' Julian put in. 'It was one of those cases of casting bread on the waters, etc.'

'Well, I was a bit longer than I expected

getting stamps and finding a place for lunch. It was about ten past twelve when I got to the porch and found Julian wasn't there. I thought she must have gone back to the café, and was just making for it when an old woman bobbed up and launched a volley of Italian at me which I couldn't follow. She kept pointing at the cathedral door and I managed to make out *"signora inglese,"* and tried to get in, but couldn't. Then the old girl gesticulated madly and finally grabbed my arm and led me to an official-looking house, and rang the doorbell. The outsize cleric Julian was talking about answered it, listened to her, and by amazing luck turned out to speak quite good English. He produced a key on the same scale as himself and came over with me.'

'But how odd that if the old woman knew Julian was inside, she'd let the sacristan lock her in.'

'Probably he wouldn't have listened to her. She obviously wasn't *persona grata* with the cathedral people. I expect they didn't care for begging on their doorstep, possibly at the expense of their collections.'

'Anyway, she won't need to beg for quite some time,' Julian said. 'We saw to that before we left.'

The conversation moved on to details of police activities after Julian's release. The Strodes had been asked to stay at Portrova overnight, and to leave their addresses both in Venice and London. But they had heard nothing further. At the time they got the impression that the police suspected certain local unemployed.

'Of course the detailed knowledge of the cathedral's layout and routine points to locals,' David added.

Pollard, who had been unusually silent, turned to Julian.

'Tell me,' he said, 'did the chaps smell?'

She looked surprised.

'Smell of what, Tom?'

'Well, unwashed humanity. Or cheap foreign cigarettes or booze or petrol. Anything.'

'I don't remember noticing that they did. But my cardigan was over my face, and now you mention it I remember its clean woolly smell. I'd washed it before we came away.'

'But one of them had his hand over your mouth and nose, you said.'

'Yes, he did at first, till they got me away from the door. But I don't remember noticing that it smelt of anything special, though.'

'Interesting,' Pollard commented.

Chapter 1

Katharine Ridley slammed the car door and sank into the passenger seat with a gasp.

'Never,' she said emphatically, 'never *never* blurt out a mad idea that comes into your head in a committee meeting. Look what I've landed us with. I really am sorry, Francis.'

Francis Peck, Warden of Fairlynch Manor, a Heritage of Britain property, gave her an amused glance as he let in the clutch.

'Not to worry,' he said. 'If other HOB places can make a success of exhibitions, why not us? Look how well Earlingford did with that Victorian children affair. Their admissions simply shot up last year.'

'Oh, I know. I'm just having an attack of guilt and cold feet at the thought of all the wear and tear ahead. But even at this moment I can see that it could be enormous fun. Anyway, calling it "Pictures for Pleasure" is an inspiration, don't you think? Not too highbrow, and subtly flattering to lenders and patrons. And we can put in more or less anything we like.'

26

Two years earlier, after agonizing deliberation, John and Katharine Ridley had made over Fairlynch Manor and its well-known gardens to the Heritage of Britain Council. Within a month of the final transfer, John Ridley, an apparently robust sixty-five, had had a fatal coronary. With her world fallen about her ears Katharine had carried out the plans they had made for their old age. The lodge of the Manor and a manageable area of garden had not been included in the deed of gift, and as soon as the necessary alterations had been made to the little house, she moved in with her orphan granddaughter Alix Parr. And being a realistic if impulsive woman, she schooled herself resolutely to keep clear of the new management and refrain from anything that could possibly be construed as interference.

A situation swiftly developed which she had never visualized. She found herself on effortlessly easy terms with Francis Peck, the newly-appointed Warden, a dedicated conservationist, absorbed in his job and quick to realize the value of her detailed knowledge of the Manor and its gardens. Her relationship with his wife Hilary was equally happy, and for the first time since John's death it seemed that life could once again have a measure of form and purpose. Her only disappointment had been the inevitable delay in opening the Manor itself to the public. The gardens had always been the priority, and with rising costs the attractive Regency house had suffered. Much needed doing to it in the way of repairs and redecoration, and a self-contained flat had to be made for the Warden.

'Well anyway,' Francis Peck said as they waited at traffic lights, 'this means we'll have to push on a bit with the house to be able to have the library ready for this affair by April. You'll feel we're moving at last, won't you?'

'I know I'm maddeningly impatient,' Katharine admitted, 'and you're so long-suffering when I try to hustle. But look, getting the library finished won't delay work on the house as a whole, will it? That would be a disaster.'

She turned and looked at him anxiously. Her alert face was heart-shaped with high cheekbones, bright blue eyes and a small beaky nose. At sixty she looked younger, with hardly a wrinkle and only a powdering of grey in her crisp hair. Quick in movement, she was full of vitality.

'I've been thinking about that,' Francis Peck replied, characteristically quiet and deliberate. 'I don't see that it need. The library and hall must jump the queue, but as we shan't admit people to the rest of the house, work can go on there all through the summer, and on the semi-outside jobs like putting in the new boiler.'

As they left Wellchester behind and headed westwards, they went on discussing plans for the projected exhibition of paintings. At the Area Committee it had been agreed to keep this as far as possible on a basis of local ownership, asking people to loan pictures from their homes which they enjoyed looking at. A further suggestion had been to offer limited hanging space to the Wellchester Art Club, offering exhibitors facilities for selling their work.

'The really vital thing is to get Hugh Rossiter to help,' Katharine said. 'It's luck having an artist of his standing in the village. And through his art shop in Wellchester he must be well up on who can paint in the Club, and who round here owns what and might be persuaded to lend it. I hope to heaven he isn't going off on a painting trip just now.'

'Isn't he President of the WAC?' Francis Peck asked. 'He might get them to lend us canvas screens for free. There isn't all that amount of hanging space in the library.'

As they talked, a bend in the road brought the village of Spireford in sight, its houses strung out along a terrace above the river Spire, here making its way northwards in leisurely silver sweeps. Fairlynch Manor stood on a southwest facing hillside just beyond the village, in a woodland setting which on this sunny November morning was a mosaic of copper, gold and bronze, interspersed here and there with the emphatic dark greens of conifers. At the sight of the low white house Katharine felt a now familiar pang. She had come to it as a bride, and in it the pattern of her life had unfolded through nearly forty years. And there, just below the lowest terrace of the garden, on the path leading down to the road and the water meadow, she had found John lying on that autumn morning...

The car ran through the village and turned in at the drive gates. The lodge was just inside on the right. As Francis Peck drew up, the front door opened, and a small white and tan dog erupted with a continuous high-pitched yodel of welcome. A young girl in blue jeans and a scarlet pullover dived after him, grabbing him just in time to save the car door from delirious scrabbling.

'Shut up, Terry,' she adjured him as he

struggled in her arms. 'Did you have a puncture or something? You're frightfully late.'

'No mishaps,' Francis Peck said, getting out and going round to open the passenger door for Katharine. 'It was the meeting. It just went on and on.'

'On and on,' Katharine reiterated, extracting herself and her belongings. 'I'm sorry we're so late, Alix darling. You must be starving. We both are, and stunned into the bargain. I'll tell you about it over lunch. No use asking you in for a quick one, I suppose, Francis?'

'Thanks awfully, but as we're so late I'd better push on before Hilary and Kit have scoffed all the lunch.'

'Kit?' Alix Parr asked quickly. 'Is he down for the weekend?'

'Just for tonight, and a bit hipped at finding himself involved in the Gilmores' gathering. By the way, can we give you two a lift, Katharine?'

'That would be marvellous. Really, I'm becoming a transport parasite these days, but it does seem silly to take two cars, and it would be such a squash in mine.'

'Wait till I pass my test next year,' Alix said. 'I'll develop my road sense by giving everybody lifts.'

'I'll hold you to that,' Francis Peck told her, getting back into his car. 'Will a quarter to seven, do you, Katharine?'

He drove off up the drive with a parting wave. Alix slipped her arm through her grandmother's and they went into the house. A pleasant smell of hot food greeted them.

'Lunch is all lined up,' she said, with a touch of conscious competence. 'I've concocted a casserole. Lamb chops, onions, carrots, potatoes – the lot. Apple charlotte to follow. Shall I bring it in?'

'Marvellous!' Katharine sniffed appreciatively. 'Yes, do, darling. I won't be a second.'

The lodge had been solidly, if unimaginatively rebuilt at the turn of the century. Katharine had enlarged the living room by extending it at the back. The result was a good-sized pleasant room with its main window overlooking the Spire valley. Here, with a selection of furniture and pictures from the Manor, she had felt unexpectedly at home from the start.

Today Alix had put up a gate-legged table in the window through which sunshine was streaming in.

'Much nicer than eating in the kitchen on a day like this,' she said, depositing hot plates in front of her grandmother. 'Now do tell me what's up. Nothing dire about the Manor, is it?'

Katharine peered into the casserole.

'Darling, you've done this beautifully... Let me help you, first... Well now, the whole thing really is that HOB says we simply must step up admissions next summer. They're spending the earth on the house, as you know. I had a sudden rather wild idea in the middle of the meeting, and suggested some sort of art exhibition in the library as an extra draw. Well, to cut a long story short, they all leapt at the idea, and a resolution was passed *nem. con.*'

Alix paused, a laden fork half-way to her mouth, and whistled briefly.

'But Gran, who's going to run it?'

'Francis and myself, as far as I can make out – in the first place, anyway. These are the main ideas at the moment.'...

Alix listened with the detached critical air of the intelligent adolescent, interrupting with a query from time to time.

'But are people going to want to lend pictures they like? I mean, the whole thing depends on that, doesn't it? Suppose there was a fire, or a burglary or something.'

'It seems that you can insure things in

exhibitions,' Katharine replied. 'There are people on the Area Committee who know all about that sort of thing, and they said it would be all right. We aren't likely to be offered priceless Old Masters, of course. As to persuading people to lend their pictures, I'm banking on getting Hugo Rossiter involved. If he puts in some of his own, I'm pretty sure the idea will catch on.'

Alix glanced across the room at the portrait which hung over the fireplace.

'What about "The Young Heir"?' she asked with a grin.

'Of course we shall lend him. He'll be the centre-piece of the whole show if I have any say in the hanging. We might have you sitting underneath,' Katharine added teasingly.

'Wot, me be a gimmick? Not even for HOB.'

Frederick George Matravers Ridley had inherited the Fairlynch estate in 1800 at the age of eighteen. Now removed from his ancestral home to the lodge, he contemplated his new modest surroundings from a massive ornate frame with an appraising air. Copthorne had painted him in the typical garb of a member of the landed gentry of his day. His rich crimson waistcoat and snowy muslin neckerchief showed to advantage under a short black coat. His faultlessly styled wig had two neat rows of curls over the ears. The papers in his right hand had been a subject of speculation to his descendants, some maintaining that they were the Fairlynch rent roll while others suggested a draft of a proposal of marriage to the heiress whom he ultimately and very profitably led to the altar.

The resemblance between Alix and the portrait was remarkable, and the subject of frequent comment which tended to irritate her. She had his broad face with its slightly pointed and determined chin, his deep brow and fine wide-set eyes. In addition, her face in repose had the same thoughtful and questioning expression of the young Ridley of the portrait. All these were Ridley characteristics, and although sometimes dormant for several generations, they tended to recur with remarkable fidelity.

'All right, we'll let you off that,' Katharine said. 'Heaven knows, there'll be enough to do in dozens of different ways. Now, I haven't told you about the Wellchester Art Club idea. The Committee think it would arouse a lot of interest if we let them have some hanging space, and told them they could sell anything they exhibited. Of course Hugo would be invaluable... Alix, you're miles away. Not even listening.'

'Gran, I've just had a super idea!' Putting down her spoon and fork with a clatter Alix pushed her empty plate to one side. 'Let's have a St Crispin section. The kids do masses of art to liberate their hang-ups, you know. It'd be a terrific boost for them to have something on show. Kit Peck's school had an exhibition last year, and he says it did marvels for duds and anti-social types.'

Katharine reacted with instant exasperation.

'My dear Alix, the idea is to attract more visitors to Fairlynch. Maladjusted children's daubs are hardly likely to do that, are they? We need money.'

'Everything's always money when it's people who ought to count. They're what matters.' Alix relapsed into an adolescent sulk, her elbows on the table.

'Is that fair?' Katharine demanded, her impatience gaining the upper hand. 'Running places like St Crispin's costs the earth, and who foots the bill? People like us out of the exorbitant taxes we have to pay... Have some more apple charlotte,' she went on, steadying herself, and heartily wishing that the argument had never started. 'No? Well then, shall we clear up lunch? I'd better get on with the herbaceous border while the light's good enough. What are you doing this afternoon?'

'Oh, I'll come and lend a hand,' Alix mumbled after a brief pause. 'I got my history essay done while you were out.'

As she collected plates and cutlery Katharine thought unhappily that while each of them had made a gesture it was once again merely an agreement to differ. Over the past year or so, while coming to realize that living without John could still have meaning and even times of happiness, she had for the first time encountered life's irony. Now, while busy in the kitchen, she struggled to keep normal conversation going, but at a deeper level her mind moved restlessly between her daughter Helen, Alix's mother, who had utterly rejected her home and its values and died tragically, and Alix herself, already showing disquieting symptoms of rejection on quite different grounds. And this in spite of an upbringing planned to avoid a repetition of Helen's disaster...

She surfaced to find Alix staring at her with a puzzled expression.

'Are you feeling O.K., Gran?' she asked awkwardly.

'Quite, thank you, darling. Just a bit tired after that endless meeting in a hot stuffy room. Let's get out into the fresh air.'

The garden of the lodge was sheltered and felt pleasantly warm in the slanting rays of the afternoon sun. Both keen gardeners, they relaxed as they worked, watched by Terry from a supervisory stance on the wall, but Katharine was pursued by memories, sharp and vivid like brief shots on a television screen. Helen's note in her sprawling handwriting, announcing her departure to have a life of her own. The squalor of the London flat in a dubious neighbourhood share with three other girls. The series of casual visits to Fairlynch, usually with young men whose appearance, manners and general attitude to life had left John and herself gasping. Finally Geoffrey Parr, introduced as a posh car salesman, better bred and mannered than his predecessors, but so blatantly amoral and on the make that Helen's infatuation for him was utterly beyond comprehension...

'Are we going to divide up this clump of phlox?'

Alix's voice broke in on the sequence of memories, and Katharine concentrated with relief on making a decision. A fresh planting was carefully sited, and the clearance of the border taken a stage further.

'I'd better hump this lot to one of the Manor bonfires,' Alix said presently, forking Michaelmas daisies onto a laden barrow. She trundled it away up the drive, purposely followed by Terry with nose to ground.

Katharine watched her go but unseeingly, as the procession of memories relentlessly resumed its course... The long silence and the last telephone call, announcing an imminent departure for Paris, where Geoff had landed a marvellous job. The casual reference to a baby due in the summer. Then the final silence, John's abortive enquiries, and the last telephone call of all from the British Consulate... Madame Parr had died in giving birth to a daughter in a convent hospice... Monsieur Parr? But did not Monsieur Ridley know of his death two months ago?

Distant sounds of Alix's return cut into the agonizing recollection of it all. Seizing a spade, Katharine began to dig furiously.

'Do you know, I think we've done about enough for today,' she said, as the wheelbarrow reappeared with the terrier as a passenger. 'Don't you think some tea would be...'

The telephone was ringing in the lodge,

and she felt the sharp inner constriction that the sound still caused in her, even after all these years.

'I'll go.' Alix flung down a fork and was off in a flash. Almost as if she had been expecting the call, Katharine thought uneasily. Could it be Kit Peck? She mistrusted the Pecks' twenty-three-year-old schoolmaster son's influence on Alix: a do-gooder, throwing away a public school and Oxbridge education to teach in some appalling comprehensive school in a slum area. Always talking about the 'underprivileged'...

After a short interval Alix returned, grinning broadly.

'For me. My boy-friend, Charles Hindsmith.'

'Who's he?' Katharine asked, conscious of relief.

'You know, Gran. The lad who comes out to the village once a week to the Bank branch. He wanted me to go to a disco in Wellchester this evening, and was all lined up to collect me in a borrowed Mini.'

'Really, Alix!'

'Well, why shouldn't he take me out, Gran? I mean, all this country stuff is out these days. The trouble with him is that he's an awful snob himself. What the HM calls the inverted sort. He keeps on about my having posh friends he knows I'd rather go out with. You know. He's an awful bore, really. I wish I'd never changed cheques for you in the village. That's how he fell for me. He was even lurking outside school one afternoon, but I dodged him.'

'You seem to be coping with him all right,' Katharine said. 'I'll be suitably discouraging if he turns up here. Where's the small fork?'

As they cleared their gardening tools and put them away her natural resilience began to reassert itself. Perhaps after all she was worrying too much about Alix, especially in the Kit Peck context. She realized that she was looking forward to going out to drinks at the Gilmores.

Chapter 2

Malcolm and Lydia Gilmore were a prosperous and sociable pair in their early forties who lived at Weatherwise Farm, a couple of miles beyond Fairlynch Manor. They had bought the farm, sold off most of its land to neighbouring farmers, modernized the house and moved out to it from Wellchester. Both worked hard. Malcolm had built up a successful construction firm, and Lydia's knitwear boutique, Tops, had a more than local reputation. They enjoyed good living, entertained freely, and were generally voted decent sorts.

Two cars were drawn up at the front door when Francis Peck and his contingent arrived.

'Whose?' Katharine said as she got out. 'Hugo's, and Lady B-C's vintage Rolls. How old does a car have to be to qualify as vintage?'

Before anyone could give an opinion the door opened, and Malcolm Gilmore appeared under the porch light, a tall well-built man with a narrow face, thick fair hair and an assured manner.

'It's you lot, is it?' he said. 'Good. I've a bet on with Hugo that I'll identify arrivals by the sound of their engines. Come right in. Lydia told you it wasn't a party, didn't she? Just a few of us for a glass and a gossip.'

He kissed the women, slapped Kit Peck on the back, remarking that it was luck he was down for the weekend, and led them all into a large room where a log fire to scale blazed on the hearth, and there was an impressive display of drinks and snacks.

'Fairlynch,' he said. 'I'll be back in a shake. I can hear the Rectory Morris Oxford chugging up the drive. Get out your wallet, Hugo.'

He disappeared. Lydia Gilmore came forward, comfortably plump in black slacks and an embroidered mandarin jacket from Tops, her head tilted back to keep the smoke from her cigarette out of her eyes.

'Fine,' she said. 'Nice of you all to turn out. Come and find somewhere to sit. Everybody knows everybody, of course. Just a cosy little parish pump get-together.'

'Katharine,' an authoritative elderly voice demanded, 'What's all this I hear about...?'

Malcolm Gilmore's appearance with

James Preston, Rector of Spireford, and his wife, cut short the questioner.

'My score's one hundred per cent,' he announced. 'I identified the Rectory Morris before it even turned into the drive.'

The Rectory car was a perennial parish joke. Katharine asked if it could be called a genuine vintage model.

'Not vintage,' James Preston said. 'To me, vintage suggests class. Valiant veteran would be more apt, I think.'

'For God's sake, Malcolm, give people some drinks,' Lydia broke in. 'We may as well use up what we've got in the house as we're heading for the bankruptcy court... He took delivery of a Jag yesterday,' she explained to the company, 'and is car-drunk.'

There were excited exclamations on all sides. Derisory laughter came from the depths of an armchair where Hugo Rossiter reclined at ease in slacks and pullover.

'Bankruptcy my foot,' he commented. 'It's ostensibly a Gilmore Construction Limited company car, you innocents. That's how it's done. No problem!'

Malcolm Gilmore grinned.

'So what? All's fair in love and war, and I'm for non-stop war with this bloody government – sorry, padre – which never stops thinking up new ways to prevent you making a profit... I'd like to see your tax returns, Hugo... What are you all drinking? Lady B-C?'

'Can I do anything about the eats?' Alix Parr asked Lydia.

'That would be super, love. Push a couple of trolleys round a bit, and then park them where everyone can grab.'

As conversation rose, it was suddenly checked by sharp rapping on a table with Lady Boyd-Calthrop's beringed hand. An imperious dowager, she stared fixedly at Katharine Ridley.

'I absolutely insist on knowing what you're up to, Katharine,' she said raspingly in the sudden silence. 'What *is* this about an exhibition of paintings at Fairlynch next summer? Melville Bonnington rang me up about it, but as you well know, he's quite incapable of making a plain statement.'

Katharine, taken unawares, mentally blasted Melville Bonnington and the ill luck which had brought her into contact with Lady Boyd-Calthorp before the vitally important move to secure Hugo Rossiter's co-operation had been made. She felt herself going tiresomely pink.

'Oh dear,' she said. 'This is frightful. Melville is a menace: I can't think why he's ever put on committees. The plan for an exhibition only saw the light of day at this morning's meeting, and I haven't seen Francis since we got back. Naturally, the first thing we were going to do was to discuss the whole thing with you, Hugo.'

There was nothing for it but to try her personal charm. She directed an appealing semi-whimsical glance at the figure in the deep armchair. Hugo Rossiter's observant dark eyes were regarding her with quizzical amusement. So far, so good, she thought.

'Come clean, my girl,' he invited. 'Why the sudden plunge into show biz?'

'Why, Fairlynch. The HOB top brass say we've simply got to step up admissions and make more money. So I thought an exhibition of pictures or something next summer when the gardens are open might bring in more people,' she concluded simply.

Hugo Rossiter gave a shout of laughter.

'Pictures or something! Anything that'll bring 'em through the turnstile, in fact! What a woman!'

'Now don't be beastly to me, Hugo,' Katharine retorted. 'You know I'm better at getting things done than putting them into words. If you'll only listen, I'll tell you all that was decided this morning!'

'Not at all a bad idea,' Lady Boyd-Calthrop adjudicated briskly. 'If Heritage can get the library useable in time, of course,' she added, looking severely at Francis Peck.

'Just one small point,' Hugo Rossiter said. He stretched out his legs, clasped his hands behind his head and contemplated Katharine. 'Where are the exhibits to come from?'

'Well, Hugo dear,' she replied, catching a few eyes and slightly raising an eyebrow, 'to begin with, Francis and I thought that being President of the Wellchester Art Club, you could easily get them to exhibit, especially if we let members make sales.'

Malcolm Gilmore, circulating with a bottle in each hand, hooted loudly.

'The trap's closing, old man! You'll be running the show yourself before you know what's hit you.'

'Art for art's sake,' Hugo retorted. 'You wouldn't understand... All right, Katharine, you scheming woman. I'll handle WAC. But let me tell you all, there'll be a selection committee of one – me, and not a single twee peep of Old Wellchester will get by.'

There were protests.

'All I can say is that if you don't appreciate Old Wellchester, a lot of people do,' Lady

Boyd-Calthrop told him. 'And if you're simply going to hang up a lot of washy watercolours by local people, Katharine, I call "Pictures for Pleasure" a thoroughly misleading name for this exhibition.'

Under cover of the laughter sparked off by this remark, Hugo winked at Katharine.

'Dear Lady B-C,' he said. 'How marvellous you are at hitting the nail whang on the head. The same idea has just occurred to me. So what, Katharine, love?'

I've landed him, she thought with relief…

'It's really quite simple,' she said. 'We're just going to ask people round here to lend us the pictures from their own homes that they enjoy looking at. Only just for the summer, of course.'

There was a moment's surprised silence.

'Well, I'll be – blowed!' Lydia Gilmore exclaimed with admiration. 'To look at you, nobody would think you had such nerve, Katharine! It's a marvellous idea, making people pay to look at their own property. Of course, we'll lend you anything you like from here, won't we, Malcolm?'

'I vote we make a start with Jacob's coat of many colours in glorious technicolour then,' Hugo Rossiter said promptly, indicating a large abstract in arresting colours which hung over the mantelpiece. 'It'll fill up a whole chunk of wall.'

'I daresay it isn't to your highly cultivated artistic taste,' Lydia replied. 'I know I know nothing about art, but – yes, I'm going to say it – I do know what I like. You arty types are such snobs. Those colours are super. They give me ideas when I'm buying for Tops.'

He gave a groan and buried his face in his hands.

'I think it's super, too,' Alix said. 'Do have it, Gran. Smashing colours. It's somehow exciting.'

'I'm all for the beer can boys over there,' Kit Peck said, pointing to an angular painting of a bar scene in which the drinkers' bodies were composed of empty beer cans. 'It's got something.'

Katharine looked at his serious face in astonishment.

'You're absolutely right, young Peck,' Hugo Rossiter said with approval. 'It's called "Thirst". An ex-miner did it, who was entirely self-taught. The empty cans symbolise the psychological reaction of a chap walking into a pub, of course.'

The Prestons looked completely lost. Lady Boyd-Calthrop, who had been inspecting other pictures in the room, sniffed audibly.

'As most of the visitors will be in what are now called the older age groups, you had better have a few exhibits that they can recognise as pictures. I suggest this charming flower painting of yours my dear,' she went on, turning to Hilary Peck. 'And, of course, that religious picture over there that your great-uncle painted, Malcolm. It'll give tone. They all think it's an Old Master.'

'We simply can't! It's an awful daub,' Malcolm protested. 'People will say we don't know a picture from a tradesman's calendar.'

'Oh, but I'd like to have it,' Katharine cried. 'I think it's rather fun, especially the donkey. We need variety, don't we Hugo?'

'Anyway, it's small,' Francis Peck said, screwing up his eyes as he visualised the library. 'Even with the canvas display which we're counting on Hugo to borrow from the WAC, there won't be all that amount of hanging space.'

Hugo Rossiter sank back with a groan and closed his eyes.

'"The Young Heir's" jolly big,' Alix remarked.

'Are you really lending a family treasure like that, Katharine?' Eileen Preston asked.

The conversation turned to fire and burglary risks and insurance cover, and moved on to more light-hearted topics, stimulated by the Gilmore hospitality. People moved around and small animated groups formed. After making a hideous grimace at Katharine and a number of exaggerated protests, Hugo Rossiter settled down between her and Francis Peck and the three began to discuss a plan of campaign. Lady Boyd-Calthrop, after a brisk passage with James Preston over Series Three, discussed Fairlynch and its problems with shy and quiet Hilary Peck, for whom she had genuine affection. Kit Peck and Alix Parr inevitably gravitated together, a fact which Katharine observed. Later in the evening, while talking to the Prestons, she learnt with satisfaction that Kit Peck was not coming home for Christmas. He would be working with a team of volunteers to give down-and-outs Christmas cheer in a disused warehouse in the East End. While sympathising with the Prestons on the absence of an extra bellringer, her mind busily planned festivities for Alix. The child needed fun with contemporaries of her own sort to get her out of this morbid preoccupation with social problems. As Francis Peck drove the Fairlynch contingent home, she exerted herself to be particularly pleasant to Kit.

During the weeks between the Gilmores' party and Christmas, 'Pictures for Pleasure' began to take shape. With characteristic quiet purposefulness Francis revised the building and redecorating schedule at Fairlynch in consultation with the architect, and contacted the Wardens of other Heritage of Britain properties to get advice on the staging and running of exhibitions. Hugo Rossiter reported that the Committee of the Wellchester Art Club were eating out of his hand, delighted at the offer of hanging space and sales facilities for their members, and very willing to make a free loan of their canvas display screens. He also helped Katharine Ridley to draw up a list of possible lenders of pictures, and they were both encouraged at the response to some tentative requests. In short, everything seemed to be going so well by mid-December that it was agreed to let up on the project until after all the Christmas and New Year festivities.

Unforeseen difficulties, however, were just below the horizon of the New Year. Over Christmas itself the weather was brilliantly sunny with an exhilarating hard frost. Early in January a period of rain set in which was to break meteorological records for the time of year. A pall of low cloud settled down over the countryside, so low that wisps wreathed ceaselessly and eerily among the trees of the Fairlynch woods. The long drought of the previous summer had already created problems for the gardens, and these were now added to by waterlogged soil and paths which became water-courses. Growth seemed to be at a virtual standstill. Katharine felt guiltily conscious of having neglected the gardens owing to preoccupation with 'Pictures for Pleasure', and realised that she was in the bad books of Tom Basing, for many years the head gardener. He lost no opportunity of escorting both Francis Peck and herself to inspect particularly depressing scenes.

'Opening Day April the second?' he enquired with heavy sarcasm. 'Better make it April the first this year, I reckon. Unless folks are daft they'll stay away this season. Unless they come to see *pictures*,' he added, a wealth of meaning in his tone. 'Just take a look at this here.'

They were standing by the great bed of polyanthus on the upper terrace, normally one of the chief spring attractions. After being decimated by the previous summer's drought it had been largely replanted in the autumn, and was now a muddy expanse spotted by pathetically small clusters of leaves.

'Now cheer up, Tom,' Katharine urged. 'It won't rain for ever, you know. We've had bad winters before, we've often been amazed at the way things have put on growth and caught up.'

Her attempts at optimism were sceptically received, however, and the collapse of part of a retaining wall undermined by the non-stop rain did not improve the morale of the garden staff.

There were also unexpected crises in the Manor itself. The library walls had been replastered and were slow to dry in the damp air. To speed things up Francis Peck stepped up the central heating, and the boiler promptly broke down. It was an old-fashioned type running on solid fuel, and scheduled for replacement before the next winter by a modern oil-burning model. Frantic telephoning established that it was impossible to supply the new boiler under two months, and there was a delay of several weeks over getting a necessary spare part for the repair of the old one. Electric heaters were hastily borrowed and hired, and the prospect of the next heating bill reduced the normally equable Francis Peck to an unusual state of gloom.

The hold-up in the library was infuriating for Katharine Ridley and Hugo Rossiter. They found themselves inundated with offers of more pictures than could possibly be accepted, but until the library was clear of workmen and their clobber, it was impossible to get an accurate idea of the available hanging space, and to make a final selection. Hugo began to show signs of frustration and restiveness, and Katharine had moments of near-panic in which she saw herself left to shoulder full responsibility for the exhibition. She felt edgy, and was in a far from ideal state of mind to handle tactfully an unexpected clash with Alix. It was unexpected because the Christmas holidays had gone reassuringly well. Alix had really seemed to enjoy the numerous parties and outdoor fixtures, and the short visit to London arranged as a special treat. She had only contracted out on one occasion in order to help with an entertainment for the children at St Crispin's, and Kit Peck's visit to his parents had been so brief that she could hardly have seen him. When the spring term started, Katharine noted, she showed a healthy reluctance to get down to her school work again.

Over tea one day, a few weeks later, Alix announced that she had had to decide on the university she wanted to go to.

'You have to give three in order of preference,' she said.

'Good gracious,' Katharine exclaimed, 'decide already? Why, you won't be going up until the autumn of '79. It seems so far ahead.'

Alix sat playing with the knife on her plate.

'I've decided that I'd rather go up this year,' she said abruptly, 'as soon as I've got my A levels.'

Katharine stared at her incredulously.

'But Alix, you can't possibly! We shall be in Canada. You know that Uncle Jim and Aunt Louise are expecting us as soon as the gardens close at the end of September. We shall be in time for the autumn colours, and then there'll be Christmas with them and winter sports for you. It's been a promise ever since your grandfather died.'

'I don't want to waste a whole year messing about. I want to qualify as a social worker as soon as I possibly can, and the first thing's to get a degree.'

'Aren't you being rather selfish?' Katharine controlled her dismay with difficulty. 'Jim is my only brother – my only near

56

relative now besides you, and I see so little of him.'

Alix looked up eagerly.

'But of course *you* can go, Gran.'

'I see that you have it all arranged,' Katharine replied in cold anger. 'I suppose everything has already been discussed with the Pecks.'

'I haven't said a single word to anyone,' Alix protested desperately. 'I haven't even got the forms from school yet... Gran, you're being unfair to me. It's not that I'm not terrifically grateful to you for all you've done for me, but – but I've simply got to have a life of my own... I just can't go on living here and having absolutely everything while millions of people are having awful lives and needing help, even here in England.'

There was a lengthy silence. In a vivid flashback Katharine was in the drawing room at the Manor, confronted by a rebellious Helen making the identical demand for a life of her own. Well, she had had one – for three short years, and what a travesty of a life, poor darling... Somehow or other Alix had got to be stopped from this preposterous contracting out of the life she had been born into, and even before she had begun to live as an adult... Anyway, I must cool this argument, she thought. It's only making things worse.

'Why is there any doubt about your university?' she asked suddenly. 'Ridleys have always been to Cambridge.'

Alix relaxed, as if relieved, by the change of subject.

'Why, I'd never make Oxbridge. I'm just not in that class. I'll have to swot to get decent A levels if I'm to fetch up at my redbrick first choice.'

'Not make Oxbridge?' Katharine echoed in genuine astonishment. 'What about that girl from your school who won an Oxford scholarship last year? It said in the local paper that her father was a bus driver. I mean, she didn't even come from an educated home, presumably.'

'That doesn't matter these days if you've got real brains. She had: the sort that can do maths.'

'I see,' Katharine said untruthfully. Groping for her next move she had a sudden inspiration.

'I do understand that you want to get on with your career, Alix,' she said, 'but surely you could turn going to Canada for six months to good account? I mean, go to a

Canadian university, and perhaps get a diploma of some sort. Wouldn't seeing how things are done over there be useful experience?'

Alix, obviously taken aback, considered this suggestion with the critically appraising expression of her forebear looking out from his portrait over the mantelpiece. Slowly her face brightened.

'I never even thought of that, Gran. It's a super scheme. But would I get taken on anywhere, though?'

'I shouldn't think there'd be any difficulty if your A level results are all right,' Katharine said, feeling startled by what she had impulsively put in train. 'We can ask Jim to make enquiries, anyway.'

'But I'd have to spend a year at a university to do any worthwhile course, wouldn't I?'

'There wouldn't be any problem there. Of course I should want to get back for the summer, but you could be based with Jim and Louise. They'd simply love it. Shall I write to them?'

'Oh, Gran, do! I feel quite excited! It would be terrifically worthwhile – help! It's nearly six, and I promised Miss Benson to lend a hand with Brownies, and I'll be late.

Back about a quarter past seven.'

She dropped a kiss on the top of Katharine's head and fled. A few minutes later the front door banged. Terry returned to the hearthrug, his hopes of a walk disappointed. Katharine put down a hand and absently fondled his ears. What had she done? Suppose the plan improvised on the spur of the moment actually came off? Suppose Alix met someone in Canada and married him. Well, suppose she did? She would be of age and in control of the money John had left her. Unless it were somebody utterly unsuitable, wouldn't it be better for her than marrying Kit Peck or another of his type, and spending her life in a sort of grey twilight of social misfits? There was room to move in Canada, and scope for getting on... Being successful ... wasn't considered ... a crime ... as ... it ... was ... becoming ... here...

The insistent clamour of the telephone woke her. She frowned a little as she went across the room and lifted the receiver. She gave her number. A rather breathy and faintly non-U voice asked for Alix.

'This is Mrs Ridley speaking. My granddaughter is out. Who is it, please?'

There was a pause.

60

'It's a friend of hers. Charles Hindsmith.'

For a moment the name meant nothing to Katharine as she quickly reviewed Alix's circle. Then she suddenly remembered the conversation in the garden on the day when 'Pictures for Pleasure' had first been mooted. Obviously this persistent and un-suitable young man must be choked off.

'Mr Hindsmith?' she echoed interrogat-ively. 'I don't think I've ever … oh, yes, of course. You're the cashier who comes out to our local branch of the Southern Counties Bank, aren't you? How very late they keep you at work, don't they? Is something wrong with one of her cheques?'

'It's nothing to do with the Bank.' The voice was defensive and sulky. 'I've rung to ask Alix to come out with me tomorrow night. I've got transport.'

'To ask my granddaughter to go out with you tomorrow night, Mr Hindsmith? I'm afraid she's already engaged: we are dining out. *Good*bye.'

She replaced the receiver with satisfaction. Really, enough was enough…

Before she could return to her chair the telephone rang again.

'Francis Peck,' came a familiar voice. 'Just to let you know that the foreman says they'll

61

be through with the library in a couple more days, so it'll be the all-clear for you and Hugo at last.'

'Thank heaven!' she exclaimed. 'Marvelous news. Have you rung Hugo?'

'No, I haven't. Will you pass it on?'

'Will I not? I can't wait. Thanks most awfully for letting me know, Francis.'

A few moments later she was dialling Hugo Rossiter's number, Charles Hindsmith and his presumption forgotten.

Chapter 3

After the frustrating delay, Katharine Ridley enjoyed the hard work of the following weeks. Every picture offered on loan had already been inspected, and either accepted or tactfully declined on one of a number of convincing grounds. The next step was the accurate measurement of the available hanging space and the making of a final selection. The owners of the pictures chosen had to be contacted, and arrangements made for collection or delivery. All this took time. Finally came the actual hanging, an exhausting and lengthy operation owing to Hugo Rossiter's exacting standards, useful help being given by local members of Heritage of Britain and of the Wellchester Art Club. By means of united efforts the work was completed by midday on Friday, April the second, with twenty-four hours in hand.

The library of Fairlynch Manor was a very large well-proportioned room that had been built on to the original eighteenth-century house. It was well lit by tall windows fitted with elegant internal shutters. Access was from the rear of the entrance hall, near the door leading to the kitchen premises.

Hugo Rossiter made a minimal adjustment to the alignment of a picture and descended from a pair of steps. Standing in the middle of the room with arms akimbo he looked around with a satisfied expression.

'If you ask me,' he remarked, 'we've done a bloody good job. Glad to be back in the ancestral home, my lad?' He bowed ironically to the portrait of the young heir, which, as Katharine had hoped, formed the focal point of the exhibition, carefully sited and flanked by unobtrusive immediate neighbours.

'You two must be feeling on top of the world,' Rex Allbright, President of the Wellchester Art Club said. 'All your inspiration, Mrs Ridley.'

'I may have had the original idea,' she replied, 'but the end product's Hugo's. He's got a phenomenal visual memory. I suppose, though,' she went on a little doubtfully, 'Lady Boyd-Calthrop won't take umbrage at the sixth baronet being rather in a corner and dwarfed by Lydia Gilmore's abstract?'

'Why the hell shouldn't it be?' Hugo demanded. 'They're both meaningless exercises in technique. And if anybody suggests starting shoving things round at this stage, I'm going home to blow my brains out.'

They all turned as the door opened to admit Francis Peck and an elderly man with grey hair and beard and rimless spectacles. Katharine exclaimed with surprise and pleasure.

'Why, it's Professor Chilmark! I'd no idea you were in these parts. How nice to see you again.'

'I'm staying with friends near Wellchester,' he told her as they shook hands, 'so I thought I'd run over and have a look at this exhibition of yours. Actually I'm on my way to a luncheon engagement, but Mr Peck has kindly offered me a private view on Sunday morning.'

'Actually it's much more Mr Rossiter's show than mine at this stage,' Katharine told him. 'Of course you've both met?'

'On several occasions, haven't we, Mr Rossiter? May I say how much I admired that Umbrian landscape of yours in last year's Academy? You've got something here, I hope?'

'Only a couple of small local landscapes,

Professor,' Hugo replied. 'We've aimed at a local flavour as far as possible, you see.'

'It promises to be a most interesting show. I hope I may see you both on Sunday morning as well as the pictures? Now I really must be off, I'm afraid...'

The Professor was led away by Francis Peck.

'He's HOB's art adviser,' Katharine explained to the rest of the company, 'and very knowledgeable. He's awfully nice, and was on the small committee which came down to vet Fairlynch when my husband offered to make it over.'

Rex Allbright asked what Professor Chilmark's own line was.

'He doesn't paint much now,' Hugo Rossiter said. 'He's more of an art historian these days. You've probably heard him on the air.'

Francis Peck came in looking unusually elated.

'One up for Fairlynch. It'll go back to the Central Committee and raise our stock. We aren't the most popular property just at the moment. You *are* through here now, aren't you? Hilary says drinks are laid on in the flat, and she hopes you'll all come up. It's time to celebrate, don't you think?'

A chorus of approval and thanks greeted the invitation, and within a few minutes a relaxed and cheerful gathering had collected in the Pecks' sitting room. Their flat was on the first floor of the Manor at the opposite end of the house from the library, with a splendid view down the terraced garden to the Spire valley and the hills on its far side. Katharine Ridley, standing at a window with a glass of sherry in her hand, felt guilty but relieved. She had given little or no time to Tom Basing and his problems for weeks, but the strong north winds of the past month had dried up the soaking ground like magic, and she could see fresh green and flecks of colour everywhere.

On leaving the house she decided to make a quick tour of inspection on her way home. The general transformation astonished her, experienced gardener though she was. The woods behind the house were misty with young green. The oaks were breaking into fat lime-gold buds, and because of the lateness of the spring the ground was still spangled with primroses and violets. Early white magnolias were in bud, and best of all, a few perfect blooms of softest pink had appeared on the treasured towering camp-bellii. The polyanthus bed which had caused such despondency earlier on was showing spikes of bright colour, and as she hurried down the terraces she found a favourite scarlet japonica a mass of bloom in a sheltered corner, and caught a waft of fragrance from a clump of narcissi. On her way down the drive to the lodge it seemed that more daffodils had come out in the course of the morning. Of course the gardens were very backward this year, but so were everybody else's. Gardening enthusiasts would know that the present promise would be a glory in a few weeks' time, given a reasonable amount of sun. The azaleas would be at their best then. And 'Pictures for Pleasure' was arousing a lot of interest: admissions should certainly be up this season, she thought, slipping her latchkey into the lock. At the prospect of a free afternoon she felt herself beginning to unwind. Quite suddenly life seemed full of pleasant things: a normal amount of leisure; Professor Chilmark's visit on Sunday, the change in Alix since Jim had written so confidently about openings at Canadian universities. After a snack and a short rest she would potter happily in her own greenhouse until Alix came home for tea.

The following day, Friday, felt like a

holiday. After getting Alix off to school and doing minimal housework Katharine drove into Wellchester to have her hair done. Exhilarated by the result she paid an unpremeditated visit to Tops. On hearing her voice Lydia Gilmore emerged from her office at the back of the little shop.

'Katharine! My God, it's good to see somebody like you in the place! We've had the most frightful women in this morning. Flat as boards or with huge overhanging balconies. Is this a social call, or in the best sales jargon, can we do something for you?'

'Of course it isn't a social call,' Katharine told her. 'I wouldn't presume to make one on a high-powered business woman in working hours. No, I feel a complete mess after working about twenty hours a day for weeks, and want something new. And warm. The wind's simply Arctic, and it's going to be freezing chatting up visitors to the gardens tomorrow.'

'You would come in right at the end of the season when the winter stock's practically cleared out,' Lydia Gilmore grumbled, opening and shutting drawers. 'The only decent knitwear's Italian these days, and I don't go over to buy in for the autumn till the end of the month. What about this? No, hopeless.

Wrong colour for you... This might do. It's warm, but not bulky or hairy. Come and try it, and these others. All half-price to you. I'm sick of seeing them around.'

Katharine fell at once for a polo-necked angora sweater in a soft blue, featherweight and very warm. Lydia brushed aside her protests at the price cut.

'You're doing me a favour by taking it off my hands. And now you're going to do me another by coming out to lunch. We'll go to the grill room at the Imperial and have a really decent meal. I'm ravenous, for some reason. If I go there alone some type from the Chamber of Commerce nobbles me and starts talking about the rates and parking restrictions.'

It was an excellent lunch in a pleasant un-demanding atmosphere of chat about local affairs and holiday plans. Lydia Gilmore was envious of the forthcoming trip to Canada.

'Couldn't I do with six months away from it all,' she said. 'Running a business is hell these days, what with one thing and another. You daren't be away for long on end, even with Tops, although I try to take it as lightly as I can – I'd go round the bend otherwise. Malcolm gets so steamed up at the way the government keeps on chucking a spanner in the works. It's never-ending with all a construction firm's ramifications, you know. I make him take a short break whenever he can, but all the real holiday we had together last year was a measly ten days in the Algarve in September... Tell me, what are you going to do about the lodge if you're really off for six months?'

She looked tired, Katharine thought sympathetically. Was it really necessary for them to work so hard, even with two children at expensive boarding schools?

Saturday dawned clear and sunny, and the early weather forecast was reassuring about showers. Glancing out of her bedroom window as she dressed Katharine watched the daffodils being bowed to the ground by the relentless northerly wind, but consoled herself with the thought that the gardens were sheltered to some extent by the wooded hills behind the house.

'I'll be down in a couple of minutes,' she called in response to a shout from Alix that breakfast was ready, and went over to get her new sweater which was spread out invitingly on the top of her chest of drawers. As she picked it up the telephone extension on her bedside table rang.

As she took four steps across the room a whole range of possible disasters at the Manor rushed through her mind, but Francis Peck's voice was reassuring.

'Nothing dire,' he said. 'Just rather tiresome. Hilary's mother has had a fall and fractured her femur. She's in hospital, and Hilary feels she must go up, as her father's on his own. I'm running her into Wellchester, of course, but I've told her that we can manage perfectly well. The chief thing that's worrying her is Chilmark's lunch tomorrow. Could you possibly lay on something, do you think?'

'Of course I can, Francis. Either here or in your flat. No problem at all. I *am* sorry about all this. Do tell Hilary, and give her my love, won't you?'

'Mine too,' put in Alix, who had been following the conversation on the telephone in the sitting room. 'And Francis, Hilary was on the gate this afternoon, wasn't she? I can perfectly well do it for her. I've been on before.'

'Alix, that's fine,' he replied. 'Could you collect the float from me when I get back? I'll look in on my way home, Katharine. Many thanks to both of you. See you later, then.'

He rang off. Katharine put down the receiver with a feeling of relief.

'Thank heaven for deep freezes,' she said, arriving in the kitchen. 'I'll have to leave the later stages of the cooking to you, I'm afraid, if I'm to help show Professor Chilmark round.'

'O.K.,' Alix replied. 'Can do. Anyway, we needn't bother much about our lunch today. Not with a Gilmore supper tonight. Malcolm's fetching us, isn't he? He seems to think we'll all be flat out by closing time.'

'I only hope he's right,' Katharine said, pouring herself out a cup of coffee. 'I shall feel much better if we get off to a good start... That car which went up the drive just now has come back and stopped outside... See who it is, darling.'

The caller was a photographer from the *Wellchester Evening News,* diverted from the Manor to the lodge in the Warden's temporary absence. Katharine collected warm outdoor clothes and went with him to discuss vantage points for photographs of the gardens. Francis Peck returned, and there were some last minute arrangements to settle. With these and household chores the morning passed swiftly. After a hurried snack Alix collected her float and a picnic tea in a basket and hurried off, enjoying her responsibilities. A branch of the drive led to the visitors' car park. A summer house used as a ticket office stood at the foot of a flight of stone steps leading up to the gardens. Here she installed herself for the afternoon, unnecessarily early.

Katharine waited until half a dozen or so cars had gone past, and then made her way to the gardens. She had been encouraged to keep up her habit of being about whenever she could on open days. Both she and John had enjoyed meeting the garden enthusiasts who came to look round, and although thefts of plants were rare, they had always felt that this was probably due to their own unobtrusive presence. Today she was surprised at the number of visitors already strolling along the paths, some with nurserymen's catalogues in hand, and was soon greeted and caught up in discussions. It was some time before she could extricate herself to go and see how 'Pictures for Pleasure' was faring. As she went into the hall an encouraging babble was coming from the library. About thirty people were inspecting the exhibits, and she had a word with the Gilmores, who were just leaving. The names of the pictures' lenders were arousing a good deal of interest, and she overheard one or two ribald comments which she treasured up to retail to Hugo Rossiter. Under pressure he had reluctantly agreed to be present on the opening day, and she was amused to see him inescapably pinned down by an earnest woman in plaid trousers and an anorak. She gave him a discreet V-sign to which he responded with a scowl, and slipped out after a couple of minutes feeling exhilarated. There was an unmistakeable smell of success in the air.

People were still coming up from the car park in small groups, and Katharine wondered briefly how Alix was getting on. Among the flowering shrubs an elderly couple were admiring the white magnolias. She stopped to give them a friendly word in passing, and was asked rather diffidently if it would be possible to get a magnolia established in the small garden of their suburban bungalow. As she entered into the pros and cons she was aware of someone standing a little way behind them, obviously waiting for an opportunity to speak to her, and as they moved on with repeated thanks for her help she turned to greet the new arrival.

She found herself face to face with Geoffrey Parr.

In the disintegrating terror of an experience apparently outside the natural order she went cold. There was a long silence. At last he broke it.

'Disconcerting, isn't it, when somebody rises from the grave? I always think Lazarus must have got the frozen mitt from quite a lot of his old pals.'

She felt her brain beginning to function again although the muscles of her throat remained paralysed. The appalling thing was that the question of identity simply did not arise. Beyond any shadow of doubt this *was* Geoffrey Parr, not so much coarsened as intensified. The once humorous mouth had tightened into an ironic slit. The calculating eyes were more unwavering and now bloodshot. There was a subtle but unmistakeable suggestion of being up against life.

'The silence of utter disapproval,' he commented, as Katharine still did not speak. 'You haven't changed, have you, mother-in-law? But the set-up has, I gather. I've been getting all the gen from my daughter down there.'

Fury and fear gave her back her voice.

'You haven't…' she blazed at him.

'Introduced myself? Of course not. Many a promising situation is ruined by being over-hasty, you know. I' – he broke off at the sound of approaching footsteps – 'I suggest we meet up at your new home for a nice chat. A bit public here, don't you think?'

He turned and strolled off in a leisurely way as two women appeared from the opposite direction, and bore down on Katharine with enthusiastic exclamations about the beauty of the Fairlynch gardens. She was astonished to hear that years of practice were enabling her to make the right responses. She could feel her head nodding judiciously and her mouth smiling automatically, and knew that by some miracle she was appearing perfectly normal. At last she glanced at her watch, simulated surprise at the lateness of the hour, and managed to detach herself.

It was possible to escape any further encounters with visitors by taking a circuitous route to the lodge. As she hurried along she found that the initial shock of Geoffrey Parr's reappearance was wearing off, and that she was thinking coherently. The circumstances of his official death were, for the moment, a side issue. The important and urgent matter was the motive behind his visit. Obviously it was blackmail, probably with Alix as the bargaining counter. She was still a minor, so he could have paternal rights over her. But could a parent who was legally dead claim them? He could go to court, of course, but by the time so complicated a case was decided she would be eighteen, and of age…

In her relief at this comforting thought Katharine released a long pent-up breath. But almost at once an even more disquieting idea struck her. How would Alix, impulsive and with her over-developed sense of social responsibility, react to the sudden appearance of a father she had never known, and one who had fallen on hard times? What unspeakable folly would she commit? Somehow – at whatever cost – Geoffrey Parr must be bought off, and persuaded to leave the country.

Absorbed in these thoughts Katharine suddenly realised that she had arrived at the lodge. As she put her latchkey into the lock Geoffrey Parr came silently round from the back of the house and followed her inside, closing the door behind him. She led the way to the sitting room, sat down, and motioned him to a chair facing her own. He seated himself, and gave his surroundings the leisurely evaluating glance that she remembered so vividly from his visit to Fairlynch with Helen.

'Very nice,' he commented. 'You've made

yourself very snug, haven't you? I gathered from my daughter just now that your late husband made over the estate which was legally hers to this conservation racket called Heritage of Britain.'

Sure of her ground here, Katharine moved in swiftly.

'You are misinformed about the Fairlynch estate,' she said coldly. 'It was not entailed and was entirely at my husband's disposal.'

Geoffrey Parr crossed his legs and leant back in his chair.

'Legally, perhaps. Morally, his action looks a bit dubious to me. Was Alix, as my daughter tells me she's called, consulted at all? Too young, perhaps? I admit that she struck me as a bit immature for seventeen. She's under age, of course, so I'm perfectly entitled to take her back to London tonight.'

Katharine reacted vigorously, realising that he was probing.

'I don't think so. You are legally dead, and your French death certificate is with my solicitor. By the time you have succeeded in establishing your identity in an English court, and your claim to parental rights has been heard – I should contest it, of course – Alix will be of age.'

'Dead men do tell tales sometimes,'

Geoffrey Parr replied urbanely. 'This would be a good one, full of human interest for the Sunday papers. I admit that I walked out on Helen with no intention of going back. It was a case of hopeless incompatibility once the first fine careless rapture had faded. And she was so bloody obstinate about asking her father for an allowance. I decided that a clean break was the only solution. I changed my name – I'm George Palmer, by the way – acquired an appropriate passport, and discreetly faded out. Naturally I wasn't in the least anxious about Helen. All she had to do was to return here to affluence and the role of deserted wife with a poor little chee-ild. If she was bloody-minded enough to starve in a bedsitter, well, it was up to her, wasn't it? How she must have enjoyed the melodrama of blotting me out by identifying some poor bastard who turned up in the Seine as me.'

'Suppose you come to the point about this visit?' Katharine suggested in an expressionless voice.

'Obviously, it's a recce.' He studied his finger-nails for several seconds. 'When I left France I headed for South Africa. A delightful country in many ways. The going was pretty good at first. Lines like respectable agencies for this and that, and of course well-known possibilities on the side. The trouble is that people interested in them are apt to go over the edge and their friends get involved. Being in some respects a fly chap I thought recently that I'd better get out. So here I am, back in the Old Country, rootless and short of cash, and naturally my thoughts turned to Fairlynch and my son or daughter. I hitched a lift to Wellchester, got myself genned up on the situation out here, and boarded the Spireford bus.'

Geoffrey Parr paused again. This time he looked steadily at Katharine with malicious amusement.

'My impression of young Alix is that she'd be sympathetic. A serious-minded lass with the popular social conscience. We had quite a long chat at the ticket booth. I wonder how she'd get on with my current girl-friend? And of course she'll be coming into money quite soon, won't she?'

Appalled by his astuteness Katharine managed to fight down her rising panic by sheer will-power.

'How much do you want to clear out for good?' she said bluntly.

'Oh, come,' he said. 'Aren't you being a shade crude? I suggest a little accommodation to suit us both. Let's be realistic. You can't surely believe that I want to be saddled with a nice pure-minded young girl like Alix? Suppose we say five thousand, with a cast-iron guarantee on my part to get out and stay out this time? Not necessarily in a lump. Of course, you'll want a little time to think it over. You hold a few cards yourself, don't you? I suggest that we give it a week. As I know your address there's no need for you to know mine. But meanwhile' – he gave a mock-deprecatory gesture – 'I do happen to be a bit short at the moment.'

For the first time Katharine fully registered Geoffrey Parr's worn duffle coat and cheap mass-produced shoes. Without speaking she got up and walked across the room to her bureau, conscious of his eyes following her. He's really broke, she thought. Surely I can turn that to account?

'This is most helpful of you,' he remarked, still in the same tone of light irony. 'Not, of course, a cheque just at the moment. Notes for small amounts, if you can manage it. Although I suppose even tenners are in that category these days.'

Without speaking she counted out one ten pound, two five pound and ten one pound notes and held them out to him. He had risen to his feet, and on taking them from her, flicked through them.

'You still bank with the Southern Counties, I expect?' he asked, stowing the money in an inside pocket.

'I do,' she replied briefly.

'Well, thank you. I feel we understand each other very well, don't you? Perhaps it would be as well if I made my exit from the back door on this occasion. As I've paid the whacking admission charge, though, I'll just have a look round for old times' sake before I push off.'

She returned from letting him out through the kitchen and for a few moments stood in the middle of the sitting room seeing nothing before sinking into her chair by the fire. Through a kind of sifting process her thoughts began to arrange themselves in layers. On the surface was the immediate preoccupation of how to explain her disappearance from the Manor. It must have been noticed by now, and someone would track her down. The second priority was to get out of the supper date with the Gilmores, which she simply could not face. The excuse of a chill from standing about in the gardens on the top of being overtired after a gruelling week seemed a reasonable explanation to offer, she decided.

With this settled Katharine began to consider the much more fundamental problem of the menace of Geoffrey Parr's reappearance and attempted blackmail. Should she tackle the situation alone or consult someone whom she felt she could trust? Her solicitor, David Greenhalgh, for instance? He was an old friend and had been a tower of strength at the time of John's death. Would she be able to make him understand that at absolutely any cost Alix must be prevented from knowing that her father had turned up, because of the unpredictability of her reaction? The child's whole future was at stake... Sudden tears of desperation sprang to Katharine's eyes. Then, hearing running footsteps coming down the drive, she hastily dashed them away and tried to compose herself as the front door burst open. The next moment a flushed Alix with wind blown hair was staring at her in dismay.

'Gran! Are you O.K.? When I came up from the gate Francis and everybody were asking where you were. Nobody'd seen you for ages.'

'It's nothing really, darling,' Katharine reassured her. 'I must have got a bit of a chill inside. Such a nuisance, but I simply had to come home. I hope everything's gone all right?'

'Jolly well, Francis says. A lot more people than he expected. Except for a type who managed to get upstairs and nose round who had to be rounded up, it all seems to have gone like a bomb... But look here, you'd better go to bed and keep warm. I'll go and switch on your electric blanket. Of course I shall stay and look after you, and not go to the Gilmores.'

With some difficulty Katharine persuaded her that this was quite unnecessary, but allowed herself to be hustled off to bed and supplied with a variety of remedies.

'I shan't be late back, of course,' Alix said, appearing later at her bedside after a hasty toilet. 'They'll all understand, and be frightfully sorry you couldn't make it. Now, are you sure you've got everything? Malcolm's car's just gone up to collect Francis.'

Five minutes later the car was heard on its return journey, and Alix ran downstairs. Her voice came floating up from outside as she explained the situation. A car door slammed and the sound of the engine quickly died away.

Katharine relaxed at the relief of being alone with her thoughts. They immediately reverted to the pros and cons of consulting David Greenhalgh. An impulsive idea of packing Alix straight off to Canada flashed through her mind and was discarded as quite impractical. She was slowly coming round to a decision to ring his office first thing on Monday morning and ask for an appointment when she drifted into an exhausted sleep. The returning car woke her, and she saw with surprise from the luminous dial of the clock on her bedside table that it was nearly half-past ten. Feigning sleep, she did not stir when Alix tiptoed in and stood for a moment looking down at her. Her bedroom door closed quietly. Not long afterwards the car passed the house once more. Silence descended and she slept again.

Tom Basing, who had worked in the Fairlynch gardens from boyhood apart from the war years, was an autocratic head gardener, but one who believed in taking turns with his chaps at unpopular chores. On the following morning this involved him in riddling the central heating boiler at the Manor, and checking that its self-feeding mechanism was delivering the correct quantity of solid fuel.

This was a job which he preferred to get over and done with before his enjoyable leisurely Sunday breakfast. He and his wife lived in a cottage in the village, and soon after seven he emerged, stood for a moment sniffing the morning air and assessing the weather prospects, and set off for the Manor. He passed the lodge, noting that the bedroom curtains were still drawn, and walked on up the drive, looking suspiciously from side to side for signs of depredations by the previous afternoon's visitors. Finding none, and being obliged to admit that the daffodils were coming along nicely, he went on and passed round the east end of the house to the stable yard at the back, taking a bunch of keys from his pocket as he did so. As he unlocked the boiler house door acrid fumes greeted his nostrils. He reflected that they were always worse when the wind was in a northerly quarter, and that it would be a darned good thing when the new boiler was put in. Less work for them all, too.

It was as he stepped over the threshold that he saw a body lying on the floor with its back to him, close to the inner door which opened on to a passage leading to the kitchen, and which at the moment was shut. Immobilised for a moment in sheer stupe-faction, to his horror he recognised Francis Peck. Within seconds he had dragged his employer out into the yard and was giving him artificial respiration. But even while he did so he knew that his efforts were futile. He had done an ambulance man's training and realised the significance of the blue lips and heightened colour...

After a time he abandoned his efforts. Acting on a deep-seated instinct for seemliness, he fetched some sacks from a shed and covered the body. Then he stood staring into the boiler house, baffled by what appeared to be a large black polythene bag and a length of cord which had been lying between the body and the inner door. He finally decided against touching them or trying the door, remembering from films he had seen on the telly that the police didn't like people mucking things about, and this looked like an inquest job if ever there was one.

There was nobody in the house, he knew, Mrs Peck having been called away to her mother, the poor lady. He turned, and began to run with the heavy pounding tread of a man in his late fifties, heading for the lodge.

Chapter 4

'The chap's dead all right, and what with the theft of the pictures, it's a damn funny business,' Inspector Rendell of the Well-chester CID reported over the telephone to Superintendent Maynard. 'The local doctor'd been sent for, and he and Doc Wheatley agreed at once that it was carbon monoxide poisoning from the boiler fumes in a small unventilated space. Off the cuff, they put the probable time of death as not earlier than midnight and not later than three o'clock this morning. It's Mr Francis Peck, the warden put in by Heritage of Britain when they took over the place. On the floor of the boiler house, near the door leading into the house, there's a black polythene bag – the sort of thing people put out their rubbish in – and a length of cord. It looks as though he was trussed up and dumped and managed to free himself, but couldn't get out. We haven't tried the inner door yet in case there are dabs.'

'Who found him?'

'The head gardener, a sensible sort of bloke called Basing. He went to see to the boiler about seven-thirty. He dragged Mr Peck clear and tried the kiss of life and whatever, but it was no go, so he belted down to the lodge to phone, where Mrs Ridley lives now with her granddaughter.'

'Wasn't anybody else sleeping in the Manor?'

'No. Mrs Peck was sent for yesterday to her mother, who'd met with an accident. There's no resident staff.'

'How did you get in?'

'A side door had been unbolted on the inside and left just latched. We went through the house and there were no signs of forced entry as far as we could see, but somebody'd got into the library where there's an exhibition of pictures, and you can see that some of 'em have gone. There was a pair of steps by one of the walls. Mr Peck could have heard a noise and come down to have a look around. His flat's on the first floor. No signs of disturbance there or anywhere else in the house. Workmen seem to be making alterations and redecorating in some of the rooms.'

There was a pause as Superintendent Maynard digested this information.

'If it wasn't a break-in, somebody must have stowed away in the place,' he said. 'Easy enough with the summer season opening yesterday. I saw in the *Evening News* last night that they'd had quite a crowd. The house not being in normal occupation and a lot of builders' stuff about would make it even easier.'

'Whoever it was must have got hold of a key to the library, then,' Inspector Rendell argued. 'The lock wasn't forced and the door was half open, but no sign of a key any-where.'

'It was probably hanging on a nail by the door,' Superintendent Maynard commented acidly. 'You know as well as I do how bloody daft people are. Did you get anything from Mrs Ridley and the granddaughter?'

'They said they'd heard nothing in the way of footsteps in the drive or a car going past. There's a dog, but it hadn't barked.'

'Plenty of other ways of coming away from the house on foot, of course, if you know the lie of the land. I take the wife over there every summer to see the gardens. But there must have been a car around somewhere if pictures were being lifted. I'll get an enquiry going right away. Anything else?'

'The granddaughter seems to have been

one of the last people to see the deceased. Mr and Mrs Gilmore – he's the Gilmore Constructions chap – live about a couple of miles away, and had asked the Pecks and Mrs Ridley and the girl to supper last night. Mrs Ridley had a chill, so in the end only Mr Peck and the girl went. Mr Gilmore fetched them by car, and brought them back about ten-thirty. He dropped her at the lodge, ran Mr Peck up to the Manor, and she says she heard the car return about five minutes later.'

Superintendent Maynard grunted.

'O.K. I'll send off the mortuary van and usual support, and be along myself as soon as I can make it. Go ahead on the usual lines.'

Detective Chief Superintendent Tom Pollard heard of Fairlynch Manor for the first time late that same evening. A free Sunday had been enjoyably spent getting away from it all on his brother's farm in Sussex. The family had not returned to their home in Wimbledon until eight o'clock, with the car loaded with country produce and the twins, Andrew and Rose, grubby and fast asleep in the back. After the latter had been bathed, fed and got to bed, Pollard and his wife Jane settled down to a leisurely snack in their sitting room. Afterwards they relaxed over the Sunday papers.

'Better hear some of the news, I suppose,' Pollard said suddenly, getting up and switching on the television set.

It had already started. An obvious reporter in a raincoat appeared on the screen in conversation with an equally obvious senior police officer.

'It's understood that the police are treating the death of Mr Francis Peck as a case of homicide, Superintendent,' the reporter suggested hopefully.

The police officer's large rectangular face remained impassive. He cautiously admitted that this assumption was correct.

'Could you tell the public the circumstances which led to this conclusion?'

'At the present stage of the enquiry this would be inadvisable.'

Pollard grinned. The reporter tried a different tack.

'I believe I'm right in saying that Mr Peck's body was found at about seven-thirty this morning in the boiler house of Fairlynch Manor. Have the police made any progress so far in tracking down those responsible?'

'I am prepared to say,' replied the Superintendent, giving the impression of being about to make an enormous concession to his interlocutor, 'that enquiries are proceeding.'

Both figures vanished.

'Our reporter talking to Superintendent Maynard of the Wellchester CID,' the newscaster informed viewers cosily.

'Poor devil,' Pollard remarked, switching off and returning to his chair.

'The late Francis Peck?' Jane asked. 'Did you know him?'

'Never heard of the bloke until now. No, poor old Super Maynard. I can just picture the sort of day he's had,' Pollard replied with a gigantic yawn.

'We'd better turn in. You've got a hefty day yourself tomorrow.'

'True. There's a mass of loose ends to tie up in the Glanford case. I'll probably have to go down there.'

During the next three days Pollard was too preoccupied to be more than marginally aware that the demise of Mr Francis Peck was attracting the attention of the Press in a big way. On Thursday morning he arrived at his desk with a reasonable hope of finishing with the Glanford affair for the time being, and was annoyed to find that he was urgently required by his Assistant Commissioner. On arriving at the latter's office it was obvious that storm signals were lying. To his astonishment he was greeted by an outburst against conservationists in general and Heritage of Britain in particular. He was conscious of an almost audible click in his mind.

'Where do we come in on this, sir?' he asked, realising that the answer was a foregone conclusion.

The Assistant Commissioner slammed some typewritten sheets down on his desk.

'We've no bloody business to be coming in at all,' he retorted. 'It's this affair at one of the Heritage people's properties near Wellchester. Fairlynch Manor, it's called...'

Pollard gathered that the regrettably influential top brass of Heritage of Britain had bullied the Chief Constable of Wynshire into calling in the Yard, having apparently expected an arrest within hours of the discovery of Francis Peck's body. Even more outrageously, they had managed to pull wires at the Home Office, and a message had come through from the highest levels suggesting that an experienced officer should take over the case.

'I suppose you'd better go,' the Assistant

Commissioner concluded. 'You'll be resented and probably obstructed by the local chaps every step of the way, of course. I don't blame them, either. It looks a straight-forward local job they could handle perfectly well. Still you've nothing on hand at the moment, have you, except the tail end of the Glanford case? Push it on to somebody else, go down to this Fairlynch Manor and get things cleared up as quickly as possible, that's all. You'll want Toye, I suppose?'

'Thank you, sir,' Pollard replied, rightly interpreting the question as a grudging authorisation. 'We'll go straight down, then, as soon as I've passed the Glanford papers over. Inspector Forrest's been working on them with us and he's quite well up in the case.'

The Assistant Commissioner sniffed irritably.

'Keep me posted, then,' he said, summoning his secretary in the next breath.

Dismissed, Pollard went to collect all information that had come in from Wellchester and returned to his room.

'Here,' he said, thrusting a folder at Inspector Gregory Toye when the latter appeared. 'The Body in the Boiler House. Digest the gen, will you, and pass it on to me when we're on the road. I'll be busy with Forrest

96

for the next hour or two.'

They had worked together on all Pollard's important cases. Toye, slight, pale and serious, and wearing large horn-rims, tucked the folder under his arms.

'It'll be like old times,' he observed.

'How come?'

'There was an exhibition of pictures on, wasn't there?'

They stared at each other for a second, remembering Pollard's first big case, the springboard of his subsequent career.

'I hope our technique's come on since then,' Pollard said. 'The AC's in a hurry. Get everything lined up, will you? Say eleven-thirty for take-off.'

Toye had a gift for assimilating facts. During the drive to Wellchester he gave Pollard a comprehensive account of the set-up at Fairlynch Manor, and of the sequence of events between early on Saturday morning and the discovery of the body by Tom Basing.

'Mind you,' he concluded, 'you can't take it in properly without seeing the lie of the land. How isolated this Fairlynch Manor is, and what the access is like, and so on.'

Pollard agreed.

'We'll have to make covering the ground

an early priority. Well, it seems clear enough that whoever was on the job never meant to kill Peck. The PM report says that the knock on the head would only have laid him out for a short time, and the tying-up must have been pretty ineffective as he freed himself. Whoever attacked and dumped him could hardly have known about the boiler giving off fumes in a north wind.'

'Disgraceful, I call it,' Toye replied with unusual heat. 'I reckon these Heritage of Britain people are responsible for him dying. Having a solid fuel boiler in a confined space with no proper ventilation.'

Pollard laughed.

'"Regina v. Heritage of Britain". Put that to the AC and he'll promote you on the spot. As I told you, he's hopping mad at our having been brought in. So are the local force, apparently. All our well known charm and tact will be called for.'

'Do you think that Mrs Peck being called away decided whoever it was to have a go at the pictures on Saturday night?' Toye asked, after a pause. 'Both of 'em being on the spot would've doubled the risk of being heard. Any chance of a lead here?'

'Doubtful, I'm afraid. There were a lot of people around on Saturday afternoon –

almost certainly too many for us to find out who knew she'd gone off and who didn't. We could discover if she was usually much in evidence when the place was open. At present I'm inclined to think her not being there was just a bonus for X. He seems to have gone off in a hurry with pictures grabbed more or less at random, and may have thought she was asleep upstairs.'

They made good headway, stopping only for a hasty snack, and arrived at Wellchester police station just before two o'clock. Inspector Rendell greeted them with the basic minimum of courtesy and escorted them to Superintendent Maynard's office. Confronted by the impassive countenance seen on the television screen on Sunday, Pollard decided that a breakthrough was a priority.

'I can tell you, Super,' he said in the friendliest manner as he sat down, 'how I enjoyed the way you handled that young cub of a newsman. I saw it on the box on Sunday night.'

To his surprise the gambit paid off. The large, rather square face relaxed and its expression became canny and faintly amused.

'Saw it, did you? Mind you, I don't deny that these interviews can be useful if there's people you want to come forward, but what gets my goat is being badgered before you've had time to size up a situation.'

Pollard concurred heartily and the atmosphere thawed perceptibly.

Superintendent Maynard apologised for the absence of his Chief Constable, unavoidably delayed on the far side of the country.

'Off the cuff,' Pollard said easily, 'I can't feel that top level wire-pulling that's brought us in' – he gave an inclusive nod in Toye's direction – 'has been any more welcome down here than it has at the Yard.'

Superintendent Maynard shifted his position and rested clasped hands on his desk.

'Seeing you've put it that way, Mr Pollard, I don't mind admitting that it's taken a bit of stomaching. Why, damn it, we've only been on the job since Sunday morning, and there's been no letting up, I can tell you that. But between ourselves, the honest-to-God truth is that we've got nowhere. Maybe coming in from right outside you'll spot something we've missed out on.'

'Suppose you and Inspector Rendell take us through the preliminary report that went up to the Yard? We've been chewing it over as we drove down, trying to get our groundwork done.'

This suggestion was clearly very acceptable. It appeared that the Wellchester police had gone over the Manor with a tooth-comb for signs of a forced entry, both inside and out, but none had been found. Therefore it had to be concluded that the thief or thieves had hidden in the house. Evidence pointed to the fact that this would have been possible during Saturday afternoon when people were coming and going to visit 'Pictures for Pleasure' in the library. Concealment would have been helped by the state of rooms which were being altered and redecorated.

'No workmen around on a Saturday afternoon, of course,' Inspector Rendell said, 'but the place was full of their gear. Easy enough to stow away behind bags of cement or planks up against a wall. I don't suppose Mr Peck looked in every corner. All I can say is that we did, and drew a blank. That goes for the Pecks' flat too. Just the prints of rubber gloves in the library and on the door from the hall into the kitchen premises, and on the inside of the boiler house door and the side door out into the yard.'

Pollard asked who was responsible for locking up the Manor at night, and learnt that Francis Peck attended to this personally, and was a conscientious type to the point of being a worrier about his job. It seemed most unlikely that he would have overlooked the side door found open on Sunday morning.

'Anyway,' Superintendent Maynard took up, 'this job wasn't casual pilfering by somebody going around and trying doors on chance. We're brought bang up against the problem of how anyone got into the library at all. A new good quality mortice lock was put on the door when it was decided to have this picture show. I've had a talk with Mrs Peck, and she says her husband kept the key in use on his key ring and carried it around by day, and put the ring in the same drawer in their bedroom every night, and that's where we found it. The spare key, with various other spares like his second ignition key, was in the safe in his office, along with the afternoon's takings.'

'Any trace on either of them of a wax impression having been taken at any time?' Pollard asked.

'None, according to the forensic chaps.'

'Another odd feature of this exhibition of pictures is the rather casual attitude to security,' Pollard said after a pause. 'They must surely have been covered by insurance, and you'd think the company or companies concerned would have made it a condition that the house mustn't be left empty. Yet Mr Peck was out for over three hours last Saturday night, leaving nobody in charge.'

'That's right,' Superintendent Maynard replied. 'He was. But it's not as rum as it looks at first sight. You see, broad and long the value of the pictures they'd got there didn't add up to a hill of beans. "Pictures for Pleasure" the show was called, and local people had just lent anything from their homes that they enjoyed looking at. Why, some of the exhibits were paintings done by members of the Wellchester Art Club, people who'd taken up art as a hobby. We had a bit of luck over finding out if anything valuable was there – the sort of thing that professional art thieves might go for. A Professor Chilmark who advises Heritage of Britain about pictures was coming to have a private view on Sunday, and we roped him in. He said that apart from one portrait there was nothing in that class, and he was doubtful about the portrait being that much of a draw. It was one of an ancestor of the late Mr John Ridley, and obviously what they were after.'

'What's the evidence for that?'

'A pair of steps was in front of it. They'd been brought in from the passage leading to the kitchen, Mrs Ridley said. The portrait was hanging crooked, and the rubber glove dabs were on the frame. Professor Chilmark suggested that they might have been going to cut it out of its frame when they were disturbed by Mr Peck. It's a hefty great frame: not the sort of thing you could go off with under your arm.'

'But they did go off with five pictures, didn't they?'

'All fairly small ones. One was hanging under the Ridley portrait, on the same picture hook. You see, the room wasn't fitted up properly for art shows. This was what you might call a trial run. There's a picture rail and all the exhibits were hung from that on cords, except for the portrait which was on a chain, being heavy. We think that the one under the portrait was taken down in case they knocked against it and made a row, but in our opinion that was their big mistake. Somehow it was dropped and the glass broke off, and the noise probably woke Mr Peck. His wife says he was a light sleeper.'

'What about the other four?'

'The cord had been cut in each case. They were in different parts of the room, all small and easy to carry, and only one of any value at all, as far as Professor Chilmark could tell from the gen in the catalogue. This one belonged to the Dowager Lady Boyd-Calthrop. Worth about £500, she says.'

'I suppose the thief or thieves were too rattled after disposing of Mr Peck to wait and carry on with cutting out the Ridley portrait, and thought they'd take pot luck to cover expenses,' Pollard said thoughtfully.

Superintendent Maynard and Inspector Rendell agreed that it looked like that. Probably agents rather than principals on the actual job.

'All the same,' the Inspector said, 'you'd think a car was a must, and we've drawn a complete blank there as well as over the access to the library.'

'Are there other houses anywhere near the Manor?' Pollard asked.

'Well, there's the lodge, of course, just off the road at the drive entrance, but as I said, both Mrs Ridley and her granddaughter say they don't remember hearing a car during the night, and their dog didn't bark and wake them. The nearest village house is about three hundred yards away, as you'll see. Spireford's one of those strung-out villages with the houses along the road, and one of our chaps has called at every one of 'em and drawn a blank. Apart from that, there's only the Manor Farm on the other side of the ridge behind the Manor itself. It's down in the next valley, you might say, and only on a farm road. In the Spire valley there's the old mill where Mr Rossiter lives, about a couple of hundred yards beyond the Manor, but that's across the water meadows. Neither he nor Mr Blaker at the farm heard a car.

'What was the weather like on Saturday night?' enquired Toye.

'Quite a rough sort of night, wouldn't you say, Rendell?' Superintendent Maynard asked.

Inspector Rendell agreed, having had to get up in the small hours to wedge a window on the landing of his house.

'You could have got something there,' he said to Toye. 'The wind making enough racket in the trees along the drive to cover the sound of anybody pussyfooting past.'

Pollard listened with only part of his attention. The whole situation struck him as decidedly odd, even bizarre, and he felt that at the moment nothing further was to be gained by discussing it with the Wellchester men. This was obviously the moment to suggest going out to Fairlynch Manor and getting some local colour. It was settled that they should drive out in convoy with Inspector Rendell. He would show them the lie of the land and then leave them to it.

'That looks like the place,' Toye remarked later, as a bend in the valley road brought Spireford in sight. 'That big white house up there. Very nice position.'

Pollard agreed. In the late afternoon sunlight the shining curves of the river and the fresh greens of water meadows and woods formed an entrancing setting. In the wake of the Wellchester police car they drove through the village getting flashes of bright colour from the cottage gardens, and turned off into a drive. That would be the lodge, he thought, as they passed a small house on the right and began to breast a sea of daffodils on their way up to the Manor. Finally they drew up on a gravelled terrace outside an elegant front door surmounted by an attractive fanlight. The door opened and a uniformed constable appeared and saluted.

'Nothing to report, sir,' he said, in reply to an enquiry from Inspector Rendell, and stood aside to let them enter. Pollard walked into the hall with a sudden quickening of interest.

His visual mind had unconsciously formed

a picture of the hall of Fairlynch Manor from reading the preliminary report on Francis Peck's death, and it was turning out to be surprisingly accurate in essentials. A central staircase curved up to the right. On either side of the hall were doors leading to the main ground floor rooms, and in the rear on the left was the door which presumably shut off the kitchen premises. Close to this door and at right angles to it Pollard could see an archway. As he expected, this led by way of a short passage to the door into the library. A seal had been put on the latter by the Wellchester police. Inspector Rendell broke it, unlocked the door and switched on the clusters of electric lights which hung from the ceiling.

Pollard looked about him with interest. The shutters of the tall windows were closed and secured with bars. It was a dignified room, on the walls of which a considerable number of pictures had been competently hung. In this ordered setting various discordant features stood out. The striking portrait of a young man in late-eighteenth-century formal dress hung at a drunken angle. There were pieces of glass on the floor below it. A battered pair of household steps stood immediately in front of it. Some canvas display screens at the far end of the room had been pushed aside, and loose ends of picture cord dangled over gaps from which exhibits had obviously been removed. A pile of printed lists on a side table by the door were scattered on the floor. Over the years Pollard had picked up some knowledge of painting from Jane, a lecturer in the history of art at a London college. A brief inspection of the works on the walls seemed to him to confirm Professor Chilmark's estimate of their value in terms of hard cash. He did not feel well-informed enough to put even a tentative figure on the Ridley portrait, pleasing though he found it. He turned to Inspector Rendell.

'As far as this room goes your reconstruction seems to me bang on,' he said. 'for the moment let's bypass the problem of how X – or X plus Y – got in, and go on to the next stage. Peck must have heard something and come down. I suggest that the library door was ajar in case X had to make a quick getaway. X hears Peck coming. It's an old house and I bet the stairs creak. X gets behind the door which will give him cover as Peck comes in. Perhaps he considers making a dash for the side door into the yard, which he'll almost certainly have had the forethought to unbolt. Peck stands listening outside, hears nothing, and makes the mistake of going into the library instead of beating it back to his flat and dialling 999. X attacks him from behind, and knocks him out. The problem now is how to put him out of harm's way while the planned theft is carried through. The polythene bag brought for carrying off the loot comes in handy. X pulls it over Peck's head and shoulders and trusses him up, not very efficiently.'

At this point Pollard suddenly broke off and looked at Inspector Rendell.

'What sort of cord was it? Picture cord?'

'No. A bit thicker than that. The sort you'd tie up a fairly hefty package with.'

'It looks as though he'd meant all along to carry off more than the Ridley portrait, then. Especially if he was going to cut the painting out of the frame.'

Toye asked if the frame would have gone into the bag, and Inspector Rendell admitted that they hadn't measured them up, produced a steel tape and noted the frame's dimensions. It would just be possible to get the frame in.

'After they'd trussed Peck up, I reckon they coasted round looking for somewhere to dump him,' he said, 'and hit on the boiler house. Nice and handy, and not far. There were no signs of dragging, so two of 'em could have carried him between 'em, or one chap working single-handed managed a fireman's lift. Peck was only average height and quite lightly built according to the report. Then they'd shoot the bolt on the house side, assuming that he'd be found when somebody came to see to the boiler next morning.'

Rendell led the way through the door into the kitchen area. The door of the boiler house was only a few yards along the passage, and had a strong bolt on the inside. He shot it back, and the three men crowded in, Toye showing strong disapproval.

'Stinking fumes even now,' he said, sniffing, 'and there's hardly a breath of wind this evening.'

'It probably doesn't draw any too well at the best of times,' Pollard replied, inspecting the old-fashioned boiler.

They agreed that the place was a death trap when both inner and outer doors were shut, and emerged once more. Inspector Rendell kicked the strong coarse matting on the floor of the passage.

'Hopeless for prints,' he pointed out.

As they returned to the hall footsteps were audible on the staircase. A young man in jeans and sweater paused, and then came more quickly down the remaining steps. He had a thatch of dark hair, large horn-rimmed spectacles on a rather long nose and a pleasantly alert and purposeful expression. Inspector Rendell introduced him as Mr Christopher Peck. Pollard shook hands and expressed sympathy.

'Of course if there's anything I can do to help,' Kit Peck said, not very hopefully. 'I mean, it all seems so – so absolutely fantastic.'

'I think a short talk on the set-up here would help us,' Pollard told him. 'We could do with some filling-in, and don't want to worry Mrs Peck more than we must at the moment.'

'As a matter of fact I don't think it would worry her – not in the way you mean. Much better for her, really, than just sitting around and wondering what the next development's going to be. I'll nip up to the flat and see how she reacts, shall I?'

In his absence it was settled that Inspector Rendell should now hand over to Pollard and return to Wellchester. As the front door shut behind him Kit Peck reappeared and reported that his mother was ready to see Superintendent Pollard, so would he come up?

As they went in Pollard noted that the flat was self-contained with its own front door. He got a brief impression of a pleasant lived-in sitting room with well-filled book-cases and numerous pictures on the walls. A woman whom he placed in her early fifties, slight and rather below average height, got up from a bureau and came towards him. She was very pale and showed signs of stress, but her grey eyes under dark brows met his steadily, and she appeared to have herself well in hand. As they sat down he said a few sympathetic words.

'Thank you,' Hilary Peck replied. 'I'd like to say that I'm glad Scotland Yard has taken over, although the Wellchester police have been doing a great deal. Please ask me any questions you like.'

Aware of Kit Peck sitting protectively near his mother, and of Toye's discreet presence in the background, Pollard considered for a moment.

'I'm anxious that neither you, Mrs Peck, nor your son shall think that our main interest is the theft of the pictures,' he said. 'I know you'll understand me when I say that your husband's death was incidental to the theft, and so the best way to find out who was responsible for it is to concentrate on the theft itself.'

In response to his enquiring glance both the Pecks nodded assent.

'The first line of enquiry we want to follow up,' Pollard went on, 'is why Saturday night was chosen. Was it because the thief or thieves knew that you were away, and that your husband would be alone in the house? I understand that you didn't know this yourself until Saturday morning?'

'That's quite right,' Hilary Peck told him. 'My father rang about my mother's accident just after eight. She had fallen downstairs and broken her leg. My husband drove me into Wellchester to catch the nine-thirty London train.'

'Right. Well now, would the fact that you had gone away have got round quickly?'

'My husband rang Mrs Ridley at the lodge to ask her to take over one or two jobs, and Alix Parr, her granddaughter, undertook to be on the gate for me on Saturday afternoon. Two women from the village were up here on Saturday morning for cleaning. They went home at lunchtime and would have told their friends, I think.' Hilary Peck smiled briefly and attractively. 'I'm sure you know all about bush telegraphs in villages.'

'Indeed I do,' Pollard assured her. 'Were

you usually on the gate on Saturday after-
noons when the gardens were open?'

'Yes. It's one of my regular jobs. So people
who come fairly often would probably have
asked Alix Parr why I wasn't there. But she
might not have known who all of them were,
I'm afraid.'

'I see,' Pollard said. 'This line isn't as
promising as I hoped, then. May we go on
to security arrangements here? Inspector
Toye has the report on them by the Wellchester police, and we'd like to go through it
with you.'

Because of the comparative isolation of
the house, the Ridleys appeared to have
taken reasonable precautions against a
break-in. The front door had a Chubb lock,
bolts and a chain, the back and side doors
bolts. All ground floor windows had either
safety catches or bars, and those of the
reception rooms internal shutters. The door
from the hall into the back premises had
bolts on the hall side. The library had the
additional safeguard of a good modern
mortice lock. Pollard asked about the lock-
ing-up procedure. Kit Peck cut in quickly as
this matter was broached.

'Dad had a thing about security,' he said
abruptly. 'He locked up himself every night

and before he went out during the day if we were leaving the place empty. You can take it that any idea that he forgot to lock the library on Saturday night simply isn't on.'

'I think we can, from what we have heard of him,' Pollard replied. 'So we're faced with the problem of what key the thief or thieves used to unlock the library door. There seems no reasonable doubt that they managed to hide up in the house before it was closed on Saturday evening, but how did they have access to a key? The most exhaustive examination of the safe, and of the drawer in which Mr Peck kept his key ring overnight, has failed to find any sign of fingerprints that can't be accounted for.'

'Could they somehow have managed to have a look at the library lock earlier on, and brought possible keys and tried them? When the new one was being fitted, perhaps?'

Pollard explained that greatly enlarged photographs of the key hole and lock had shown no scratches or attempts to try out keys. He went on to question Hilary Peck as considerately as he could, and learnt that her husband had locked the library and put the key on his key ring as soon as pictures began to arrive for the exhibition.

'You see, there were workmen in the

house,' she explained, 'and he felt responsible for the exhibits. He unlocked the library each morning when Mrs Ridley and Mr Rossiter and other helpers were doing the hanging, but the last person there had to contact him on leaving so that it could be locked again. There was only once' – her voice trembled slightly – 'when he had to be away all day and left the safe key with me. I can assure you that no one else handled it, and that it wasn't left lying about.'

Pollard was reassuring. There was obviously no point in pressing her further at the moment, he decided, and after thanking her for her valuable help he and Toye were escorted downstairs by Kit.

'What the hell are you going to do next about the bloody key?' the young man burst out.

'Nothing,' Pollard told him. 'When you come up against a "No Way" notice, the only thing to do is to try to get through by another road. We shall now go into the security arrangements at the lodge, where presumably the Ridley portrait is normally kept. Am I right about this?'

Kit Peck stared at him.

'Yes,' he said, after a moment's pause. 'But there aren't any special security precautions down there. I mean, only the sort of thing like safety catches on ground floor windows...'

'Quite,' Pollard replied. 'Thought provoking, isn't it?'

Chapter 5

In answer to Toye's ring the front door of the lodge was opened by what appeared at first glance to be the subject of the Ridley portrait in modern dress. Recovering himself, Pollard raised his hat.

'Good evening,' he said. 'I think you must be Miss Parr. I'm Chief Superintendent Pollard of Scotland Yard, and this is my colleague, Inspector Toye. I expect you have heard that the Chief Constable has asked the Yard to take over the enquiry into Mr Peck's death?'

The young girl's reaction was not one of alarm or even interest. She showed unconcealed annoyance.

'Do you want to see Mrs Ridley?' she demanded, without returning his greeting.

'Yes, please, if she is disengaged.'

'Gran!' Alix Parr turned towards a half open door. 'Scotland Yard wants to see you. You'd better come in,' she added, addressing Pollard and Toye, and backing to make room for them in the tiny hall. They deposited their hats and waited. Alix gave the door an impatient push. As she did so a woman appeared on the threshold. Pollard's first impression was of somebody appreciably older than Hilary Peck, socially confident but in a state of considerable tension.

'Gran,' Alix cut in before either of them could speak. 'I've got to take the things for supper up to the Manor. Hilary's expecting them.'

'Do you want to see my granddaughter as well as me?' Katharine asked Pollard. 'We're doing a certain amount of cooking to help Mrs Peck at the moment... I'm so sorry, I didn't catch your name.'

Pollard introduced Toye and himself once again.

'Yes, we would like a word with Miss Parr,' he said, 'but perhaps we could have one with you first while she goes up to the Manor?'

'O.K.,' came hurriedly from behind him, and the door shut noisily. Katharine Ridley was apologetic.

'I'm afraid Alix is rather on edge. This dreadful business has upset her badly. She's devoted to the Pecks. Rushing round doing things seems to make her feel better. Won't you sit down?'

As she spoke she sat down herself in a

chair by the small log fire which was burning in the hearth. Pollard took a seat facing her, conscious of Toye selecting a useful vantage point on the window seat.

'I realise what a shattering experience all this has been to both of you,' he said, 'and I'm sorry to have to bother you, particularly as I understand you haven't been well. But it's the matter of this portrait of a member of your husband's family, which seems to have been at any rate the main object of the break-in.'

As he talked he watched Katharine Ridley relax perceptibly.

'It's simply baffling, isn't it?' she said, life and warmth coming back into her voice, 'that anybody wanting to steal it hasn't broken in here? There are no elaborate security arrangements whatever, and when we're away the house is just shut up and left.'

'You've put your finger on one of the most puzzling features in the case,' Pollard told her. 'You've been living here for about two years, I think? Do you go away much?'

'No, very little really. My granddaughter lives with me and is a day girl at Wellchester High School, for one thing. And I can never be away during the summer when the Fairlynch gardens are open to the public, as I'm very much involved. In the last twelve months we were away for a week in October when Alix had her half-term, and for another week in the Christmas holidays.'

'Still, plenty of time for a planned break-in,' Pollard observed, glancing up at the mantelpiece. 'I take it that the portrait usually hangs up there?'

A sudden smile lit up Katharine Ridley's face, and he sensed for the first time her vitality and charm.

'Detection!' she said. 'Yes, you're quite right. The Jan van Huysum flower painting doesn't quite hide the marks on the wall. I needn't tell you that it's a reproduction.'

'It's a very good one. But what strikes me is that the portrait would be very obvious to anyone looking in at the window.'

'I know. I do draw the curtains when we go away, though some people say it just draws attention to the fact and is a mistake.'

'How valuable is the portrait, Mrs Ridley?'

'It's insured for eight thousand. But I should add that Professor Chilmark, Heritage of Britain's art adviser, thinks that I should step up the insurance a bit because of the rise in prices at auctions over the last few years.'

Pollard considered.

'May Inspector Toye have a look at your locks and window fastenings?'

'Certainly. It won't take long in this little house … the kitchen's just across the hall, Inspector.'

'Thank you, madam.'

Toye disappeared. Pollard asked questions about any visits from self-styled dealers in antiques, while speculating about the causes of Katharine Ridley's initial tension. Presently voices and footsteps came from the drive, and he saw her frown slightly.

'At least Alix has come back promptly,' she said. 'I'm afraid she's collected our rumbustious terrier, though!'

As she spoke a fracas of barking, growling and expostulation broke out at the front door, Toye having been discovered at his locks inspection. Alix appeared holding an infuriated Terry by the collar.

'Sorry,' she said to Pollard. 'He hasn't bitten your inspector, though. Just making a row. Shut up, Terry!'

During the dog-talk which followed Pollard noted the transformation in Alix, now attractively flushed and starry-eyed. That was young Peck with her, he thought, and she's obviously smitten. Equally obviously, Gran is county and doesn't approve…

Toye reappeared, a fresh outburst from Terry was quelled, and Katharine asked Pollard if he would prefer to see Alix alone.

'No, please don't go, Mrs Ridley,' he replied. 'We shan't be more than a few minutes. It's about last Saturday afternoon. It seems probable that whoever had decided to have a go at stealing the portrait went into the house like everyone else who wanted to see the exhibition, and managed somehow to slip off unnoticed and hide. You were on the gate all the time, I gather, Miss Parr?'

'Yea. I went up a bit before two to get dug in before people started coming, and stayed till half-past five, when we stop letting people in.'

'Did you know most of the visitors who came?'

'Not most of them. Say about a third, who were friends, or anyhow people we know.'

There was no identifiable sound such as a sudden movement on the opposite side of the hearth, but some instinctive sense made Pollard glance fleetingly at Katharine Ridley. He saw that her former tension had returned.

'About the two-thirds that you didn't know, Miss Parr,' he went on in the same relaxed tone, 'did anyone among them make any special impression on you? Did anyone stop and talk to you and ask any questions?'

Alix wrinkled her brow in the effort of remembering.

'A few people asked why I was there instead of Hilary. She does the gate on Saturdays, you see. They all seemed quite ordinary. Not art thieves, I mean or – or murderers.' Her voice was unsteady for a moment. 'Then there was a man who asked about my grandfather making Fairlynch over to HOB. I didn't like him much. He was snooty.'

'Snooty in what way?' Pollard asked.

'Well, as if making over your estate to HOB or the National Trust or whatever was a stupid thing to do, I thought. He was a bit nosey, too, about what had happened to Granpa's family. I was glad when some more visitors turned up and he moved on.'

'One often gets asked about the transfer,' Katharine Ridley unexpectedly contributed. 'By people who simply can't understand why donors don't sell to the highest bidder.'

Pollard replied politely but declined this diversionary gambit.

'Can you remember at all what this snooty and curious type looked like, Miss Parr?'

'Well, he was fairly old. He wasn't wearing a hat and had some grey hairs. I remember he had a fawn duffle coat on – a pretty old one. Oh, yes, he had very thin lips.'

'Did he come in on a Heritage of Britain member's card or by paying the entrance charge?'

Both Katharine Ridley and Alix looked in surprise at Toye sitting quietly in the window.

'Oh, he paid,' Alix said without hesitation. 'A fifty pence piece, I remember. He wasn't the sort who'd join.'

'About what time did he come?' Pollard asked. 'Can you remember at all?'

'About a quarter past three, I think,' Alix replied after a pause for thought. 'Or a bit later.'

'You had a chill on Saturday, hadn't you, Mrs Ridley?' Pollard asked casually. 'Were you up at the Manor at all during the afternoon?'

'I was about in the gardens for a short time in the early part of the afternoon, and went into the house for about ten minutes to see how "Pictures for Pleasure" was doing. It was soon after that I began to feel shivery in the garden, and decided to come back here and have a hot cup of tea. I remember that I got in at ten minutes past three.'

126

'Then you had probably left the gardens before the man Miss Parr's been telling us about had arrived.'

'I must have. At all events I don't remember seeing anyone like him.'

Pollard caught the note of finality in her voice and decided to bring the interview to an end. He and Toye had risen to leave when there was an exclamation from Alix.

'I wonder if he was the man Francis turfed out?' she said.

Pressed for further information, she told Pollard that when she had gone up to the Manor at half-past five to hand in money and ticket counterfoils, Francis Peck had said that he had found a man on the stairs. There was a 'No Way' notice at the bottom of the staircase as the house was not yet open to the public, apart from the library.

'Francis said the man was jolly rude, and so he asked him to leave.'

'Did he say when this happened, or what the man looked like?'

'No, he didn't. Somebody came up just then who wanted to speak to him, and I was counting the money, and didn't think about it again till I got back here and told Gran.'

'One does get the occasional visitor who seems to make a point of ignoring notices,'

Katharine Ridley remarked as she led the way to the door.

Once clear of the lodge Pollard and Toye exchanged glances.

'Why was she so keen to play down the thin-lipped bloke in the duffle coat, I wonder?' Pollard said. 'I'm positive she was lying when she tried to prove conclusively that she'd gone home before he turned up.'

'Hard up?' Toye suggested. 'Suppose the theft of the portrait was a put-up job between them to get the insurance money?'

'That was my first reaction. All that chat about it being much easier to lift the thing from the lodge could have been to put us off the scent. But against the idea, did you notice how she relaxed the moment I began talking about the portrait? She was badly tensed up when we arrived, as if she was afraid we'd come about something else. I'd very much like to know what it was... All the same, we'll get the low-down on the lady's finances, and ask the Super to see if the chap's trail can be picked up.'

'I've been thinking about that...'

'I bet you have,' Pollard interrupted with a grin. 'Anything on wheels with an engine. Let's have it.'

'He'd got to get here and get away again,'

Toye said, unruffled. 'If he was up to something shady I don't see him risking a crowded country bus on a Saturday afternoon. He'd have come by car, like the other visitors and parked up there.' They had paused at the point where a branch of the main drive led off to the visitor's car park on the right. 'Suppose he was the bloke Peck turned out? Either he picked up his car and drove off, or if he was also the bloke who'd come to steal the portrait, he got back into the house and hid. He'd need the car later in the night. Where was it in the meantime?'

'You could have got something there,' Pollard conceded. 'The obvious place for something is often the best way of avoiding attention, isn't it? Let's go and have a look at the visitors' car park.'

They walked up a short and moderately steep length of drive flanked by trees and shrubs, and came out into a fairly level expanse on the hillside below Fairlynch Manor which overlooked a small tributary of the Spire. The surface had been asphalted and marked off into parking spaces. Pollard looked around him carefully.

'If you parked on the side next to the house you couldn't be seen from any of the windows,' he said.

Toye agreed. Here the hillside rose steeply, and only the chimneys of the Manor were visible from where they were standing. A small ticket office in rustic oak stood by a gate from which a flight of steps led upwards to the gardens.

'Suppose you'd been over to see the gardens and this "Pictures for Pleasure",' Pollard went on, 'and were one of the later visitors last Saturday afternoon. When you came down to get your car and drive home, would you pay much attention to another car still in the park? Well, I daresay *you* would. Notice its make, or even go and snoop to see what mileage it had done, but my guess is that all most people would be thinking about at that stage would be getting home for a nice cuppa.'

Toye conceded this further point.

'There's another thing,' he said, as they retraced their steps. 'The slope's downhill, all the way to the road, and the road itself's downhill for a bit going north and away from the village.'

'Meaning that anyone could coast down in neutral and get clear of the house and the lodge before starting up the engine? Yes, you could do it all right with a bit of shoving to get yourself started, I should think. And that would explain why the pair at the lodge didn't hear a car pass – if there was a car, that is. All this is theorising, of course, but it's a useful idea to have in reserve. Let's go and sit somewhere in the garden and try to clear our minds.'

They found a seat on one of the lower terraces and sat down in the last of the evening sun. The wind had dropped and the air was still, warm and full of birdsong. Fragrance came drifting across from a bed of wallflowers. Pollard stretched out his long legs, clasped his hands behind his head, and gave himself up to sheer enjoyment. A faint rustling came from a nearby hedge. Toye gave a startled exclamation and hastily drew in his feet.

'What the devil is it?' he demanded, as a small spherical brown object appeared.

'Good Lord, haven't you come across a hedgehog before?' Pollard asked with amusement. 'Flea-ridden, but perfectly harmless, and the gardener's friend. They eat slugs and whatever.'

Toye eyed the advancing hedgehog dubiously. Moving silently and at surprising speed it went past without acknowledging their presence.

'Not unlike this ruddy case,' Pollard

commented, 'which bristles all over with problems. What library key did X manage to get hold of? Why did he choose to operate on Saturday night at the Manor under considerable difficulties instead of breaking into the lodge when it was empty last January? What's the link between the ex-lady of the Manor and the mystery man in an old duffle coat who seems regrettably lacking in public spirit? Can she be near-broke and out for the insurance money for the portrait? What sort of a fence is prepared to handle anything so easily identifiable as this portrait?... There's a few problems to start with, anyway. Where shall we go from here?'

They discussed the case at some length, deciding on their priorities. Because of Mrs Ridley's odd stonewalling, and in default of a better lead at the moment, the obvious step seemed to be to try to pick up the trail of the man in the duffle coat. Some of the people viewing 'Pictures for Pleasure' in the later part of the afternoon might have noticed him, or even witnessed his ejection by Francis Peck after being caught on the stairs. Or better still, his subsequent return to the Manor to hide. On the other hand, he might have been seen in or near Wellchester during the evening. Help from the local police in questioning car park and petrol pump attendants, traffic wardens, café owners and pub landlords would be needed over this. A related issue was the state of Mrs Ridley's finances, involving a dicey interview with her Bank manager.

'Of course this entire lead may turn out a dead end,' Pollard argued, 'so we'd better get going in other directions. There are the people at that party on Saturday night, especially the chap who drove Peck and young Alix Parr home. Gilmore, wasn't he called? He was the last person to see Peck alive bar the killer, as far as we know. Then I'd like to see this Professor Chilmark's views on the art robbery aspect. Let's hope he's still around. No shortage of jobs, in fact. Let's push off now, shall we?'

They had left their car on the terrace in front of the Manor, but before getting into it they walked round to have another look at the back of the house. Beyond the top of the steps leading down to the gate from the car park were greenhouses, and in one of these a light was visible.

'It might be Basing,' Pollard said. 'It would save time to see him now. I don't suppose he can tell us any more about finding the body, but he was probably around on

Saturday afternoon.'

As they opened the door of the green-house the warm moist air was almost over-poweringly sweet with the scent of flowers. A man looked up from a sheaf of narcissi and gave them a searching glance.

'Evening, gentlemen,' he said. 'You're from Scotland Yard, I reckon?'

'Quite right,' Pollard replied. 'Chief Superintendent Pollard and Inspector Toye. Are you Mr Basing, the Fairlynch head gardener, who found Mr Peck's body on Sunday morning?'

'Yes, I am. I'll not forget it to my dying day and that's a fact. If you'd care to take a seat, sir, you'll find the bench there's quite clean.'

'We've seen the very clear statement you made to Inspector Rendell, Mr Basing,' Pollard told him. 'I don't think there's much point in going over the ground again. What we've come to ask you about is last Saturday afternoon. Were you up here then?'

Tom Basing explained that normally he did not work on Saturdays, but always put in an appearance on Opening Day. He was on duty in the greenhouses and at the shed where plants were sold to visitors.

'We've had reports of a chap whose movements we're interested in, and wonder if he came along here. Someone about your age. No hat, and wearing an old fawn duffle coat. A bloke rather given to nosing about.'

'Ay, I saw a chap that matches up to that,' Tom Basing replied with a gleam in his eye. 'He stood about, sizing the place up as if he was planning to make an offer.'

'Can you add anything to the description I've given you?' Pollard asked with sharpened interest.

Tom Basing reflected, leaning against the bench at which he had been working.

'Clean-shaven,' he said at last. 'Bit bloated. I reckon he lifts his elbow. Thin lips – a mouth like a rat trap my dad would've said.'

'This is our chap all right. Lucky for us that you're so observant, Mr Basing. Now, can you remember what time it was when you saw him?'

This proved more difficult. In spite of the late spring and the cold wind there had been a surprising lot of visitors. Coming and going all the time, and old friends wanting to talk about their gardens, and what to buy to fill in the gaps left by the '76 summer drought. Finally Tom Basing thought that the chap must have been around somewhere between a quarter and half-past four.

'When did you knock off yourself?'

'Five-thirty, we close the greenhouses and plant stall. Say another ten minutes shutting up. Then I went up to the Manor to hand in the money I'd taken for plants to Mr Peck... God Almighty, do you reckon the bastard who did for him was hiding somewhere in the place all the time we were talking?'

'It looks rather like it... That's a very beautiful spray you've made. It's for Mr Peck's funeral tomorrow, I expect?'

'That's right. It's the family's tribute. Mrs Peck asked for me to do it. When Mr Ridley went, 'twas in the autumn, two years back last November, and we gave him chrysanthemums. Our own, of course... A real tragedy it was, his going so young.'

'You've been here a long time, haven't you?' Pollard asked.

He learnt that Tom Basing had come to Fairlynch as a gardener's boy on leaving school in 1934, returning after his war service and working up to be second gardener. Then in 1960 Mr Ridley, doubtless with his plans for the future of the estate, had fixed up for him to work at Kew for a year, and soon after his return he had taken over as head gardener. Mr Ridley had been one in a thousand, Tom Basing averred, and his lady was another. And when Fairlynch was handed over to Heritage of Britain you couldn't have had a nicer gentleman put in charge than Mr Peck. A gentleman who knew his job, and how to leave alone people who knew theirs and let them get on with it.

Pollard led the conversation round to Mrs Ridley, but nothing but praise of her was forthcoming. It was quite a step down from living at the Manor to living at the lodge, Tom Basing said, and everybody admired the way she'd taken the change, and was still ready to help in the gardens just as she did when Mr Ridley was living...

'After all that,' Pollard remarked as they drove back to Wellchester, 'it's difficult to imagine Mrs R involved in some shady business with a dubious-looking stranger. All the same, I'm pretty certain she did meet the chap on Saturday afternoon, and if so, why lie about it? Did you notice that it was *after* Alix had said that he arrived at the ticket office at "a quarter past three, or just after" that Mrs R stated that she'd got back to the lodge at ten past? It ought to be quite easy to get the names of a few people who were in the exhibition, say between two forty-five and three o'clock, and try to check up when she left.'

Inspector Rendell was out when Pollard

and Toye arrived back at Wellchester police station, but they were informed by the duty sergeant that Superintendent Maynard was in his office, and could see them if it would be helpful.

'No hard feelings, apparently,' Pollard muttered *sotto voce* as they were escorted along the corridor. 'Our personal charm must have worked.'

Drinks were produced from a cupboard, and Superintendent Maynard listened with unconcealed interest to an account of the ground covered during the visit to Fairlynch, his eyebrows rising slightly at the suggestion that Mrs Ridley could be involved in anything questionable. When Pollard's narrative came to an end there was a short pause during which the listener was obviously debating something in his mind. Finally he thumbed through some papers on his desk and selected one.

'I don't suppose this report that's come in from Brynsworthy ties up with your bloke in the duffle coat,' he said rather defensively, 'but there's no harm in passing it on. First of all, we had the usual joy-ride car thefts here on Saturday night. Both the cars were found abandoned in the neighbourhood, one in Brynsworthy, and none the worse expect petrol used. Brynsworthy had a car pinched sometime between eight and ten: the owner can't put it nearer than that. It was in a head-on collision with a lorry on the London road, and the driver was killed outright. There were no passengers.'

Pollard was gripped by overwhelming if wholly unjustifiable certainty.

'What time was the smash?' he asked, as casually as he could.

'Ten thirty-three,' Superintendent Maynard replied. 'Like me to ring Brynsworthy for further details?'

Details of the dead man were quickly forthcoming. He was five feet eight in height, with dark hair beginning to go grey, dark eyes, a ruddy complexion and thin lips. His clothing included a well-worn fawn duffel coat. A passport recently renewed by the British consul in Johannesburg gave his name as George Palmer, his age as fifty-one, and his birthplace as London. He had entered Britain six weeks earlier, but no address in this country was on him. He was carrying twenty-six pounds and some loose change in various pockets, the money including one ten-pound and two five-pound notes. He had no luggage of any kind. He had been drinking, and the alcohol content of his blood was above the permitted level for the driver of a motor vehicle. Enquiries into his identity were proceeding in this country and in South Africa.

Pollard, who had been listening in on an extension, put down the receiver, and grinned at Superintendent Maynard.

'Thanks for yanking us off a wild goose chase before we waste any more time on it. Soon after ten thirty on Saturday night Francis Peck was just being dropped at Fairlynch Manor by his host, having said goodbye to Alix Parr at the lodge a few minutes earlier, according to your report. And according to the PM he didn't die before midnight at the earliest.'

Superintendent Maynard, plainly gratified at his own acumen in passing on the report from the Brynsworthy police, grinned in response.

'Who'd be a poor bloody policeman?' he asked.

Chapter 6

'As we've been barking up the wrong tree ever since we got going,' Pollard remarked as he and Toye returned to their temporary office, 'we'd better have a go at another one. As I said earlier on, I think a chat with Heritage of Britain's art adviser bloke might pay off. Let's see if we can run him to earth.'

The telephone number of Professor Chilmark's friends near Wellchester was in the case notes handed over by Inspector Rendell. Pollard put through a call and found that the art expert was still with them, although leaving for London on the following day. An invitation to drive over with Toye after supper was accepted.

By tacit consent the case was given a break as they had their own meal. Pollard devoted the surface layers of his mind to a crossword puzzle, while Toye perused the columns of used cars for sale in the *Wellchester Evening News*. Afterwards there was a brief encounter with newsmen who were lurking in the hotel lounge. By a quarter to nine the

Rover was on the road heading for the village of Great Westcombe, ten miles to the south of Wellchester.

The house where Professor Chilmark was staying was easily found, and they were greeted by an elderly man with a neat beard and impressively high forehead. He escorted them to his host's study borrowed for the occasion, where a selection of bottles had been set out in readiness.

'I thought you people might contact me,' the Professor said, pouring out drinks after enquiring into preferences. 'Not that I can be of much help, I'm afraid, beyond what I could tell Inspector Rendell when I went over all unsuspecting to see the exhibition on Sunday, as previously arranged. Is it in order to ask if anything came of the Yard's enquiries into the activities of known art thieves over the weekend?'

'Quite in order,' Pollard replied. 'The answer is nil. All the likely lads can be crossed off the list.'

Having provided his visitors with their drinks, Professor Chilmark came and sat down.

'Cheers,' he said, raising his glass. 'From your tone I deduce that you, like me, are not surprised?'

'Not in the least. The lack of expertise stands out like a sore thumb, doesn't it? A highly unsuitable painting to fix on, unnecessarily difficult circumstances for carrying out the job, and sheer blind panic when interrupted.'

'My own sentiments exactly, Superintendent. I thought Inspector Rendell's reaction was an interesting one: seconds acting for a principal. The snatching up of a mixed bag of portable pictures before making off looks rather like an attempt to justify anyway a reduced fee, to my mind. But on the other hand, an experienced crooked dealer would surely have employed more competent people. And no dealer who knew his stuff would want to get involved with a portrait of that sort.'

'This is one of the things we'd like to talk to you about,' Pollard said. 'Just how valuable is this Ridley portrait, and how saleable?'

Professor Chilmark put down his glass and settled back in his chair.

'At the present moment it's insured for eight thousand. Last Sunday I advised Mrs Ridley to raise the cover to ten thousand, partly because auction prices are still rising, and partly because of all the public interest in the portrait that has been aroused. Of course, auction prices are always unpredictable, but if she put it on the market at the moment, I should expect it to fetch ten thousand at the least. This answers your question in terms of cash value, and saleability at public auction or to a private purchaser. What a fence would pay for it is a different matter.'

'What fence would handle it?' Pollard asked. 'It's easily identifiable, surely, and there's no question of who it belongs to.'

Professor Chilmark looked at him speculatively.

'It's certainly easily identified – you're quite right. It's a good example of Copthorne's work. Not of his highest achievement in portrait painting, perhaps, but good enough for favourable mention in standard studies of his work. And it is known to have been commissioned by the Ridley family and in their possession ever since. I grant you all that.' He paused. To Pollard's surprise a mischievous and slightly coy expression came over his face. 'I'll come clean, Superintendent,' he went on. 'I read detective fiction – selectively, of course. The solutions sometimes seem farfetched, but in a good yarn they are perfectly sound logically. And if the long arm of coincidence gets a bit over-stretched, well, astounding coincidences do happen in real life.'

Pollard grinned.

'Are you suggesting that we start hunting for a missing heir, sir, who finds that the non-entailed estate has been made over to Heritage of Britain and decides to annexe the best remaining chattel?'

'Missing heirs have been rather overdone,' Professor Chilmark replied. 'Readers tend to be on the look-out for them. Seriously though, Superintendent, this Fairlynch business is so odd that it's difficult to see it as a straightforward art robbery with an unintentionally tragic outcome.'

'Two possibilities that have occurred to me,' Pollard said, 'although I haven't had time to follow them up, are that the whole thing was a rag that went wrong, or that it was the work of a rabid anti-conservationist. More or less a crackpot, I mean.'

'I think that second idea is perfectly tenable in theory. I can tell you from my connection with HOB how intense anti-conservationist feeling can be. It's usually involved with commercial interests, of course, but sometimes politically motivated.'

'And in the individual it arises from

psychological maladjustment sometimes, doesn't it? There was that chap who took a hammer to the Pietà in St Peter's, for instance.'

'Quite. I suppose it's possible that there's somebody who had a violent irrational objection to an art exhibition at Fairlynch. Or somebody who has been nursing a deep-seated grievance against Mrs Ridley for years.'

Pollard experienced a sharp mental jolt. The relationship between Mrs Ridley and the man in the duffle coat which had dropped out of his mind abruptly reinstated itself. Not that the chap could have attempted to steal the portrait himself...

Professor Chilmark had got up to refill their glasses.

'I expect there are quite good collections of pictures in some of the stately homes in these parts?' Pollard asked suddenly with apparent irrelevance.

Professor Chilmark glanced up enquiringly.

'Yes, there are. At Earlingford, for instance, and at Firle Hall.'

'You've seen them, and met the owners?'

'I have. On several occasions at Firle, the Boyd-Calthrops' place.'

146

Pollard sat for a moment frowning in concentration.

'I'm thinking about your suggestion that somebody with a grievance against the Ridleys might possibly be involved in this affair. It would be useful to get the low-down on the family history of recent years. Unobtrusively if possible, in the course of conversation with a chatty member of their social set.'

'Well, of course, if that's what you want, old Lady Boyd-Calthrop's heaven-sent,' Professor Chilmark replied, returning once more to this chair. 'She's the dowager, and lives at Firle Dower House. What she doesn't know about the gentry and nobility of the neighbourhood could be written on a postage stamp. And you've got a perfectly adequate pretext for calling on her.'

'On the grounds that her exhibit in "Pictures for Pleasure" was one of those the chap carried off? That's quite true. What does it say about it in Inspector Rendell's report, Toye?'

'"Head of an Old Peasant",' Toye read, after a brief search in the case file. '"Arthur Cadell. Oil. *c.* 1890. Property of the Dowager Lady Boyd-Calthrop. Estimated value £500 10 x 8 inches approx."'

'She'd be lucky to get it,' Professor Chilmark remarked. 'I remember her showing it to me. The technique was mediocre, but the artist had managed to convey a bucolic quality – sagacity, and robustness. She picked it up for a tenner in a sale somewhere, she told me.'

'That's briefed me nicely,' Pollard said. 'Many thanks, and for all your help. Very good of you to see us on your last evening here.'

'Not at all. I've been most interested to meet you – I was in the Wrexham Gallery last week, and stopped to have a look at the "Blue Bonnet" which you retrieved so neatly just as it was about to board a plane for the US at Heathrow.'

They reminisced briefly about Pollard's first big case before he got up to leave with renewed thanks.

Toye, whose strong preference was for material clues and their methodical investigation, was openly sceptical during the drive back to Wellchester. He pointed out with perfect truth that apart from showing that she was unwilling to discuss the chap in the duffle coat, there was nothing whatever so far to link Mrs Ridley with him, discreditably or otherwise. Anyway, he was dead, and the idea that he had commissioned some-body to steal the portrait while he himself cleared out in stolen cars wasn't supported by one single known fact.

'All right, old Feet-on-the-Ground,' Pol-lard retorted amicably, 'but you've got to admit that known facts are a bit sparse at the moment. Apart from questioning all the people at the party on Saturday night, which we'll do tomorrow, there's not a single definite lead to follow up. We'd got it all worked out to ask for help from the local force in tracing Duffle Coat's movements after he left Fairlynch, and then dropped the scheme when we knew he was dead. We'll simply resurrect it on chance.'

Toye fair-mindedly if reluctantly admitted that at least this step could do no harm. On arriving at the police station Pollard put in his request, to be passed to Superintendent Maynard on the following morning, and they compiled a report of the enquiries so far made before deciding to call it a day.

Before turning in Pollard rang Jane and conveyed by an agreed code that the going was sticky. The brief contact with home was cheering and his hotel bedroom comfort-able, but unusually for him it was some time before he could detach his mind sufficiently from the case to get to sleep. The problem of the library key kept presenting itself, and when he succeeded in ousting it he was at once confronted with the enigma of Katharine Ridley's behaviour. Was her chill genuine, he wondered? Was it essential for her to be on her home ground on Saturday night as a result of Duffle Coat's appearance? And – the two problems suddenly coalesced – was it possible that she had a key to the library, retained from when she was living at the Manor, and had somehow been forced to hand it over? His feeling of relief at having at least visualised further lines of enquiry was so great that within a few minutes he was asleep.

Thursday morning was off to a good start. Superintendent Maynard was cooperative over the matter of enquiries by his men, and Malcolm Gilmore was going to be at his office all the morning, and would see Superintendent Pollard at any time.

The premises of Gilmore Constructions were at a new industrial estate on the outskirts of Wellchester. The buildings gave the impression of a successful business but one without any attempt at pretentiousness, and Pollard and Toye were impressed by the orderly appearance of the area used for storage of basic building materials. Inside the main block they found light and airy conditions and an attractive if workmanlike décor. Their arrival was reported by telephone, and within a few minutes they were escorted to Malcolm Gilmore's office by a brisk pleasant young woman who introduced herself as his secretary.

It was a moderately large and sunny room, with wall-to-wall carpeting, a knee-hole desk and comfortable leather armchairs. There was a vase of daffodils on the desk flanking a photograph of a woman and two boys in their early teens. Photographs of a variety of buildings presumably erected by Gilmore Constructions hung on the walls, and there were plans on the table in one of the windows. As Pollard and Toye came in, a tall fair man, very spruce in appearance, got up from behind the desk and came forward with hand outstretched.

'Chief Superintendent Pollard?' he said. 'I'm sorry you had to wait. It was a phone call. Do sit down.'

'I'm afraid this must be an inconveniently early call, before you've had a chance to deal with the morning's mail,' Pollard said, as he and Toye took a couple of armchairs facing the desk, and Malcolm Gilmore occupied his own chair in a relaxed, unofficial manner.

'Please don't apologise,' he said. 'It's up to the public to give you all the help it can at any time. I needn't say that anybody who knew Francis Peck is absolutely knocked flat by what has happened.'

'I can believe that from all I've heard about him,' Pollard replied. 'We've come along to you, as I expect you've already realised, because barring whoever tied him up and put him in the boiler house, you appear to be the last person who saw him alive.'

Malcolm Gilmore shrugged unhappily.

'Yes, I realise that. It makes me feel quite ghastly, in case I might have done something to prevent it. What can I tell you that might be useful?'

'Did you go to "Pictures for Pleasure" on Saturday afternoon, Mr Gilmore?' Pollard asked.

'Yes, I did. My wife and I looked in for a short time, say about a quarter of an hour.'

'We'd like you to think back and tell us everything you can remember about this visit, especially the people who were there at the time, and anything in the least out of the ordinary that may have struck you.'

Malcolm Gilmore abruptly pulled open a drawer and brought out a silver cigarette box.

'Sorry,' he said. 'I seem to be missing out on even the most basic hospitality. You don't? Neither of you? Neither do I. Well now,' he went on, sitting back in his chair with his arms folded. 'Let me think. I know we left home just after half-past two. We live about a couple of miles from Fairlynch, so we must have arrived in the car park about a quarter to three. We were surprised to find Alix Parr in the ticket office instead of Mrs Peck. By the way, have you met Alix yet, and her grandmother, Mrs Ridley?'

Pollard nodded affirmatively. 'Yes, both of them, thanks.'

'Right. Alix explained about Hilary Peck having had to go off to London because of her mother's accident. We were both disappointed, as we'd invited the Pecks and one or two other people to supper to celebrate the opening of "Pictures for Pleasure" – some damned hard work had gone into getting the show ready, I can tell you. I suppose we talked to Alix for two or three minutes, and then went on up the steps into the house. Am I giving you too much detail?'

'No. This is just what we want. Carry on as

you are.'

Malcolm Gilmore paused for a moment, tilting his head back a little. Pollard studied the long narrow face and strong chin, and waited.

'I can't swear to it, but I don't think there were new arrivals right on our heels at the ticket office, or following on. The library was quite well-filled. There must have been two dozen people going round looking at the pictures. We collected our catalogues – duplicated sheets, actually, to save expense – and chatted to people we knew as we went round ourselves. Lydia – my wife – fell for a picture put in by a member of the Well-chester Art Club, and bought it. Club members were allowed to sell their stuff. I didn't think much of it myself, but it's a good thing to encourage local talent. She wrote a cheque for £25, and gave it to the woman in charge of the catalogues. Bad luck, really, as it was one of the pictures stolen that night. Purchases can't be removed until the end of the exhibition, you see... Well, we saw everything, and did a bit more nattering, and then left. We went straight home without going round the gardens. It was hellishly cold, and they aren't at their best yet, and as we're so near, we can go anytime.'

'Thank you,' Pollard said, 'you've given us a very clear picture. Did you know most of the people who were there?'

'Not most of them, no. People come from far and wide to see the gardens. Do you want the names of the people we talked to?'

'Any that you can remember, yes. There could be a matter of timing here.'

'Well, Francis Peck, of course. He was there, and so was Hugo Rossiter, the artist, and Rex Allbright, the current President of the Art Group. A couple we know called Haversham from here, and another called Bright from Spireford village... I think that was all ... oh, I'd forgotten Mrs Ridley. She came in from the gardens where she'd been showing people round, just as we were leaving.'

'What time was that?' Pollard asked as casually as he could.

'Just on a quarter past three. I'm sure of that as I wanted to get back for a programme on the box, and had been keeping an eye on the time.'

'Did you see anyone – either in the library or the car park or anywhere – who struck you as a bit of a misfit? A rather down-at-heel male?'

Malcolm Gilmore looked interested, and

on the point of asking a question, but apparently thought better of it.

'No,' he said. 'I'm quite sure I didn't.'

'May we go on to the evening now?' Pollard asked. 'We'd like the same sort of detailed account of that.'

'The meal was planned for eightish, with drinks first. I left to collect Francis and Mrs Ridley and Alix at about a quarter past seven, and drove up to the Manor first... Now wait a bit, just let me think... I drew up outside the front door and gave a couple of toots on the horn to let Francis know I was there, and then went on about twenty yards to where you can turn. As I came back he was coming out of the door. I can see him quite clearly in my mind, slamming it shut, and then locking it and putting either a key or a key ring into an inside pocket ... I'm prepared to swear this. I mean there's no question of him having left the door on the latch by mistake.'

As he spoke Malcolm Gilmore glanced at Toye who was making entries in a notebook on his knee.

'Inspector Toye's getting all this down,' Pollard reassured him. 'Just carry on, giving us all the details.'

'Well, then we drove down to the lodge to

156

pick up Katharine Ridley and Alix. Alix came out and told us about Katharine's chill, and we talked about it for about a minute as she got into the car, and then I drove off. We must have arrived at the farm about a quarter to eight, and...'

'Just a minute,' Pollard interrupted. 'What other guests were there?'

'Only one. Hugo Rossiter, and he'd already arrived. It was really a small celebration for Katharine and him. They'd done practically all the work over "Pictures for Pleasure", as I said just now. Both he and Lydia were naturally very disappointed about Katharine. It was a bit damping to be two short, especially as Lydia had made a special effort over supper, and Katharine's vitality would make anything go. However, Hugo's good fun, and so was Francis in a quiet way, poor chap, and we had quite a successful evening.'

Pollard asked if Francis Peck had seemed in any way preoccupied or worried.

'Not in the least. He was in very good form, and jolly pleased at the way the Fairlynch summer season had started off.'

'He didn't seem anxious to get home?'

'No, I'm sure he didn't. It was Alix who said she didn't want to be late back because of her grandmother being under the weather. She's a jolly nice kid. A bit over-serious, perhaps, but it's not a bad failing these days, is it? We began to move about ten. My wife wanted to pack up some of the food for Alix and Francis to take home as there was a lot left over, so that took a few minutes. Hugo Rossiter said he'd plenty of grub on hand, and went off ahead of us by about five minutes. Then I drove back to Fairlynch, dropped Alix at the lodge and saw her in, and then ran Francis up to the Manor. We talked for a couple of minutes about the work...'

'What work, Mr Gilmore?'

'The alterations and extensions this firm is doing at Fairlynch. Then he got out, and I turned the car as I did before. When I passed the door he'd got it open and was just going in. He gave me a sort of mock salute, and – well, that was that. I drove straight home.'

There was a brief silence as Pollard thought over the facts he had heard.

'About the work, Mr Gilmore, that your firm is doing at Fairlynch. You've had men up there for some time now?'

There was a flash of anger in Malcolm Gilmore's eyes.

'On and off for about eighteen months,' he

replied curtly. 'Heritage of Britain are having a good deal done. But if you're suggesting that any of them could be involved I can only say that I sent hand-picked men up there. In any case, I've so far managed to keep a damn good work force together in spite of the bloody unions.'

'I'm making no suggestion whatever that any of your men are involved,' Pollard replied equably, 'but we're up against an extremely baffling situation about access to the library last Saturday night. Let me explain...'

As Malcolm Gilmore listened the aggressiveness in his face gave place to concentrated attention. Finally, he abruptly shifted his position, resting his elbow on the desk and cupping his chin in his hand.

'It's a snorter, isn't it?' he said thoughtfully. 'Surely there *must* have been another key somehow? But all I can say is that I simply can't see any of our chaps seeing far enough ahead to take an impression of the new library key *before* the pictures started arriving, and Francis started carrying it round on him. I mean, they just aren't in the careful planning criminal class, and wouldn't have known what to do with the Ridley portrait if they'd got it. I could get a list of every man jack who's worked at Fairlynch since Heritage took over, if you like, but quite honestly, I think this is a nonsense, Superintendent.'

'I'm inclined to agree with you,' Pollard said, 'but as you say, this problem of the key is a snorter, and we've got to look into every possible explanation. We'd be grateful to have that list. If it should ever seem necessary to check up on anybody on your payroll, we'd inform you, of course.'

'Thanks,' Malcolm Gilmore replied. 'That's an attitude I appreciate. Is there anything else I can do? By the way, can I offer you a cup of coffee? I usually have one about now.'

Pollard declined politely on the grounds of other commitments before lunch, and shortly afterwards brought the interview to an end in a relaxed and friendly atmosphere. Back in the Rover which they had left in the Visitors Only section of the car park, they studied Toye's notes of the conversation with Katharine Ridley on the previous day.

'Let's recap,' Pollard said. 'Alix Parr, who seems a reliable lass, gave Duffle Coat's arrival at the ticket office as a quarter past three or a bit later. After she had said this, Mrs Ridley stated that soon after leaving the picture show she came over queer and went

160

home, arriving at ten minutes past three. Now we have Gilmore, who had his eye on the time because of a telly programme, saying that Mrs Ridley came into the show just on a quarter past three. Presumably they at least passed the time of day, and he didn't say that she left with them, or on their heels. So what?'

Toye concluded that it looked as though an attempt had been made to mislead them about the time.

'I reckon you're right about trying to get the chap traced,' he said.

'Magnanimous, that's what you are,' Pollard remarked. 'Come on. We're due at this boutique place of Mrs Gilmore's in ten minutes. We go over much the same ground in a chatty way while watching out for any discrepancies over times.'

Tops occupied picturesque premises in one of Wellchester's narrow medieval streets, and Toye had difficulty in finding a parking lot within reasonable walking distance. They arrived ten minutes late, and Lydia Gilmore was involved with a customer.

'I won't keep you more than a few minutes,' she said, ushering them into a small office at the back of the shop. 'Sorry there isn't much room.'

They cautiously removed boxes of knit-wear from two upright chairs and sat down, gazing about them. In spite of its untidiness the office gave the impression that the boutique was doing well. There were piles of expensive-looking cardigans and sweaters on a sheet on the floor, and a number of exotic evening blouses on stretchers hanging on hooks along one wall. As Pollard remarked that it was just as well that they didn't cater for bottoms as well as tops, there was a sound of departure from the shop and Lydia Gilmore hurried in.

'Sorry,' she said once again. 'I don't feel somehow that this is a very suitable milieu for an interview with Scotland Yard, but it's all I've got.'

Pollard reassured her while apologising for being late himself, and registering the tweed skirt and toning jumper she was wearing for Jane's information at a later date.

'We won't keep you long,' he promised her, and proceeded to take her over much the same ground that had been covered with her husband.

She answered his questions with a spontaneity which convinced him that she had not been primed over the telephone after his departure from Gilmore Constructions.

Anyway, she wouldn't have listened, he thought. Her account of the visit to Fairlynch on Saturday afternoon was identical with her husband's in all essentials, and included diverting touches about the clothes worn by some women visitors to 'Pictures for Pleasure'.

'Standard wear for Wellchester Art Club members,' she told him. 'Navy blue slacks, sensible shoes and scarves and mud-brown anoraks, except for the one or two who come here, of course.'

'Such as Mrs Ridley, I expect,' Pollard suggested with a smile.

'Actually she's not a member, but certainly wouldn't look like that if she was,' Lydia Gilmore replied briskly. 'No, she came in from the gardens just as we were going, looking absolutely Lady of the Manor in a very well-cut sheepskin coat. It was freezing in the wind on Saturday.'

'It was getting late, too, I expect,' he hazarded.

'Oh, no. We went early as I had this supper party to get ready, and Malcolm wanted to view some programme. We came away about a quarter past three, actually.'

Katharine Ridley's absence from the evening's celebration had clearly been disappointing. Lydia spoke with warmth of her amusing gaiety on such occasions.

'She's a great person,' she said. 'She's got tremendous zip and courage, and dignity too. I always think the way she's stepped down from Fairlynch to living at the lodge without showing the least disgruntlement or self-pity is splendid. And she's straight as a die, too.'

Pollard brought the conversation round to the break-up of the supper party, but learnt nothing new. Alix was a good kid and obviously hadn't much liked leaving her grandmother in bed, so they hadn't tried to persuade her to stay after about ten. It seemed the obvious thing to send some of the left-overs back with her for Professor Chilmark's Sunday lunch, and to make Francis take some, too, as he was on his own. Katharine had been cooking for him, actually. No, Francis hadn't seemed in the least depressed or worried during the evening – quite the contrary, poor darling.

'So your guests departed in a body,' Pollard remarked.

'Well, not quite. Hugo Rossiter went a bit ahead as he didn't want any food. He's enslaved a widow woman from the village who looks after him and does him proud. All perfectly respectable, incidentally. His life is compartmentalised. Then Malcolm ran the others back when we'd got the food and a bottle of bubbly to perk up Katharine loaded into the car. It didn't take him long. He was back before eleven, and actually helped me finish clearing up... Yes, Sonia, what is it?'

A young blonde and with-it assistant put her head round the door and goggled slightly.

'It's the police station, Mrs Gilmore. They want to speak to Chief – Chief Superintendent Pollock.'

'Pollard,' said Lydia Gilmore with asperity. 'Why is it that these girls simply never get a name right?' she added as the blonde head hastily vanished. 'There's the phone on the desk. Shall I clear out?'

'No need for that,' Pollard replied, reaching for the receiver. He was being called by Inspector Rendell.

'We've been trying to get you,' the latter said. 'Something rather important: You'd better come back to base, we think, Mr Pollard.'

Chapter 7

'Some at least of the pictures nicked from the exhibition at Fairlynch have turned up,' Superintendent Maynard informed Pollard and Toye as they arrived in his office. 'Young Mr Peck rang in about twenty minutes ago.'

Pollard was briefly disconcerted. He realised that he had taken it for granted that some local contact of the man in the duffle coat had been unearthed.

'Have they now?' he said, straddling an upright chair and resting his arms on its back. 'Where? This could be useful.'

'They were found in a shed at the top of the Fairlynch woods, Mr Pecks says,' Inspector Rendell told him. 'He asked for you, but as you were out he gave me the gen. It seems there's a fence along the top of the ridge behind the house, a wooden posts and wire affair. The slope down on the far side belongs to the Fairlynch estate, but it's let to a farmer called Hayes who uses it for grazing. Basing had noticed that the fence had been damaged by a branch being blown down on it last week, and he told one of the young chaps who work under him to go up and repair it this morning. After he'd been on the job for a while the lad felt like having a fag and went into the shed to get out of the wind. He looked round for something to sit on, and saw what he took for a black polythene bag full of garden rubbish. He gave it a kick, found that there was something hard inside, and opened it to have a look.'

Pollard groaned in anticipation. Toye gave a disapproving click of his tongue.

'That's right,' Superintendent Maynard took up with heavy irony. 'He yanked out some pictures, and wondered what they were doing there. Then after a bit something stirred in what passes for his mind, and he remembered the pictures on show at the Manor, and somebody having got in and pinched some, and the boss being found dead in the boiler house, and decided that he'd better take the ones he'd found down to Basing. Of course when he got back he couldn't find Basing, and the Manor was locked up: they were all at the funeral at the crematorium here. So he took the bag of pictures into one of the greenhouses, and sat on guard beside it until Basing reappeared. Young Peck was fetched and had the sense to ring us. By then it was just on twelve.'

Pollard looked at his watch. It was now twenty minutes to one.

'We'd better go out and get the bag, and run it back to be gone over for dabs, if you can fix that for us. Print the oaf who handled it and the pictures, and I suppose whoever did the hanging for the exhibition. We can get that from Mrs Ridley: the show seems to have been her brain-child. The pictures will have to be done too, of course.'

'We can send someone out with you in a police car to bring the stuff back at once,' Superintendent Maynard offered. 'It would save a bit of time.'

'That would be fine, Super. Another thing, have you got a large-scale map of the Fair-lynch grounds? It looks as though this shed could be on a handy exit route from the Manor?'

An Ordnance Survey map was produced, and Pollard and Toye were on the point of leaving when Superintendent Maynard picked up a couple of newspapers.

'Seen these?' he asked. 'They've got on to the car crash.'

The Monitor had a short paragraph reporting the crashing of a stolen car near Brynsworthy. This repeated that its driver, killed outright, had been carrying a British passport recently renewed at the British Consulate in Johannesburg which gave his name as George Palmer, his age as fifty-one and his birthplace as London. A description of the dead man was given. The paragraph ended with a request to anyone knowing his address in Great Britain to contact the police. *The Flashback* had devoted two columns to the accident under the heading 'Mystery Man George Palmer'. It gave no additional information, the known facts being generously padded out with speculation of a somewhat sensational type.

'This is fine,' Pollard said, perusing both reports. 'It ought to bring in something, over and above the phone calls from Lands End to John o'Groats by people who'll imagine they've seen Palmer. But of course your chaps are our best bet for picking up his trail, Super,' he added tactfully.

Over sandwiches in a bar he studied the inch-to-a-mile Ordnance map of the Spireford area with Toye.

'Manor Farm,' the latter said. 'Down in the valley on the far side of the Fairlynch ridge, and on a farm road which comes out on the road from Spireford about a mile north of the village. Easy enough to cut up through the woods, dump the pictures in the shed, drop down to the farm road and out to a pick-up car waiting where it joins the road from Spireford. A posts and wire fence wouldn't be any obstacle, and anyway it was down in one place. And it was full moon last Monday, so there'd have been enough light Saturday night.'

Pollard sat frowning and absently rotating his glass.

'I'll buy all that,' he said after a pause, 'but you've got to remember that Rendell's boys haven't been able to find anybody who saw or heard a car on that road in the small hours of Sunday morning. Suppose the original idea was to take the portrait down to Manor Farm for the rest of the night, and get it away later? What about this man Hayes? As a tenant farmer of Heritage of Britain he'd come up to the Manor to pay his rent, and discuss repairs and whatever. Could he have somehow managed to take an impression of the library key? Peck might have been called away from a conversation they were having in his office, and left the safe open where the spare keys are kept, or his key ring on the desk. It doesn't sound in character, I admit, but people do slip up.'

Toye concluded that something of this sort was a possibility, and agreed that Hayes' activities from midday onwards on Saturday had better be looked into.

'Also his finances and local reputation,' Pollard added.

'If Hayes is X,' Toye went on, 'surely his wife must know about it? I suppose he could have had an accomplice for the actual robbery, though.'

Still frowning, Pollard shifted his position and rested his arms on the table.

'What's so infuriating about this ruddy case is the way we have to keep switching to a fresh lead before we've followed through the one before. The Mrs Ridley–George Palmer business is still in mid-air, and we haven't interviewed either her and young Alix or the artist bloke Rossiter about the Gilmore's party on Saturday night. And there's still the problem of the library key, and why the hell whoever wanted the portrait didn't break into the lodge when it was unoccupied in the Christmas holidays, and make off with it then.'

'What do you think's behind dumping the pictures in the shed after taking the trouble to nick them?' Toye asked after a pause.

'It seems to me that there are several possible explanations. It was a lunatic move to snatch up a collection at random like that, and X may have thought better of it by the time he'd sweated up to the top of the ridge with them. The hut was a handy place to drop them. On the other hand, he may have expected to be able to pick them up later. It's important to remember that at this stage he hadn't a clue that Francis Peck was going to die as a result of being locked in the boiler house, and that he himself would be facing a homicide charge. So he wouldn't have expected Fairlynch to be swarming with police the next day. And then, as I said, at Professor Chilmark's, there's the possibility that the whole business started off as a rag or some crackpot protest gesture, and that there was never any real intention to steal either the Ridley portrait or the other pictures, the idea being to annoy either Mrs Ridley or Heritage of Britain.'

'You mean that the pictures in the shed were meant to be found.'

'Yea. Even if the grounds weren't searched, they'd have been found by Basing on his next tour of inspection, of course. Here, we'd better get cracking. The chap who's coming out with us will be waiting.'

As the two cars drew up outside Fairlynch Manor, Kit Peck appeared in collar and tie. Pollard got out and apologised for having to carry on with the enquiry on the day of the funeral.

'It's O.K.,' Kit replied. 'I came down because I thought the HOB people were arriving. Two of the Central Committee were at the funeral, and they're due here this afternoon to discuss temporary arrangements for running the place, and my mother's plans. They're being very decent to her... You'll have come about the pictures Bill Manley found, I expect? We've got them locked up in one of the greenhouses with Tom Basing on guard. Shall I take you round?'

He led the way round the side of the house. Tom Basing emerged from a shed looking constricted in his best suit. The polythene bag containing the pictures was carefully enclosed in a larger one to protect any fingerprints on it.

'Did you handle it at all, Mr Basing?' Pollard asked.

'No, sir. There'll only be Bill Manley's prints on it, and the chap's who put the pictures in it. You'll be wanting to take Bill's?'

Pollard replied in the affirmative, and a stentorian bellow produced a round-faced youth with china-blue eyes and ragged fair hair.

'I've told Manley he'd no call to go fingering the bag and the pictures, but he did right to bring it down and keep the other chaps off it,' Tom Basing said, combing censure with defence of a subordinate in the presence of a third party. 'Now you'll have to have your own prints taken, Bill, so that these gentlemen can sort 'em out. Look sharp, now.'

Bill Manley vanished into one of the greenhouses with Toye, and Pollard turned to Kit Peck.

'We needn't keep you any longer,' he said, 'and thank you for ringing so promptly this morning. But we'd like some more help from Mr Basing, and then to go up to the shed with Manley.'

Kit Peck went off in the direction of the front of the Manor, and Pollard asked if there was a path up to the shed.

'Not to say a proper path,' Basing replied. 'Just a rough track through the woods, and it's half hidden under fallen leaves and such. And if it's footprints you're thinking of, I came down it myself last Friday, and Bill Manley's been up and down again this morning, trampling it.'

Toye and the youth reappeared, and a

sample of the latter's fingerprints was handed to the waiting constable to be taken back to Wellchester with the pictures. Basing suggested that the gentlemen might like to take a seat in the greenhouse, same as they had before.

'You get on with your work till you're wanted,' he adjured Bill Manley.

When they were settled, Pollard began by enquiring what the shed was used for.

'Nothing much,' Basing replied. 'Tell the truth, I've wondered what it was put there for, but seeing it's there, we keep it in repair. There's just a few oddments in it like some spare posts and coils of wire for the fence, and one or two planks and bits of rope. We keep a folding ladder up there for small jobs on the trees, but if anything more's needed in the way of tools or materials we take it up. There's no lock on the door: only a staple and hook.'

Toye asked if visitors to the gardens went up to the shed.

'Well, there's nothing to stop 'em if they've a mind to, but it's a pull up and I don't reckon many get there. Kiddies do now and again, for I've found sweet papers inside.'

'About this broken fence, now. When did you discover it?'

'Last Friday morning,' Basing replied without hesitation. 'Friday mornings I go right round the place to see what wants doing, so as I can get the next week's work straight in my head, see? The wind was something terrible last week, and I wasn't surprised to find a branch down. It had landed on the fence up there, knocking a couple of posts sideways and buckling the wire.'

'Did you go into the shed while you were up there?'

'Yes, I did, to see if there was enough wire for making good, and there was nothing that shouldn't have been there then.'

'Did you go up again, or send somebody else up, between last Friday morning and this morning?'

'No, sir, I didn't. In the ordinary way I'd have sent Manley up Monday morning to put the fence straight, but everything being upside down because of the robbery and Mr Peck's death, I didn't get round to it. It's been like that all week, and still is,' he added pointedly.

'We won't keep you much longer, Mr Basing,' Pollard assured him. 'We just want to check up on the chance that whoever was here on Saturday night went off over the hill and down the other side to a waiting car.

The land over there is let to a Mr Hayes, isn't it?'

'That's right. The farm – Manor Farm, it's called – is down in the valley, on a farm road leading to the road from Spireford.'

Pollard made a show of interest.

'There'll be dogs, of course. If a stranger was around in the small hours of Sunday morning they might have barked and woken somebody. What does the Hayes family consist of?'

'Jim Hayes himself, a chap of about forty, his wife, and five kids from round sixteen downwards. And Jim's mother lives with them. She's a widow. Jim took on the farm when his dad died, five years back I think it was.'

By way of comments on the advantages of continuity in running a farm, Pollard elicited the information that Jim was a good farmer and not afraid of work. Mr Ridley had thought the world of him and his dad. After this there seemed little point in pursuing the subject further, and he asked if Bill Manley could be summoned to go up to the hut.

'We'd like a first-hand account of exactly how he found that bag of pictures this morning. There's no need for you to come,

Mr Basing. We've taken up enough of your time as it is. By the way, have you ever seen this man in the village, especially during the last few weeks?'

Tom Basing took the glossy photograph of an unprepossessing thug from Brixton, studied it carefully and shook his head.

'If a chap looking like this'd been around the village, I'd have heard about it right enough,' he said emphatically.

Pollard carefully returned the photograph to an envelope which he replaced in his wallet.

'One more thing,' he said. 'After you had paid in the money from the sale of plants to Mr Peck on Saturday evening, what did you do next?'

'I went off home.'

'Which way did you go?'

'Down the steps to the car park, and down the drive to the village.'

'This next question is rather important, Mr Basing,' Pollard told him. 'Take your time. How many cars were still in the car park when you went through?'

'None at all,' Tom Basing replied without hesitation. 'I don't need any time to answer that one. I'd have noticed if there was any. It would've meant there was still folk around in the gardens. We don't admit visitors after half-past five, but we don't clear 'em out either, more's the pity. You never know what they might be up to, pinching the plants and suchlike.'

Asked to call Bill Manley, he went to the door of the greenhouse and gave another powerful bellow, under cover of which Pollard commiserated with Toye on the exploding of his idea of an escape car having been left in the park.

Bill Manley emerged from a shed and advanced reluctantly.

'Take these gentlemen from Scotland Yard up top,' Basing ordered, 'and tell them what they wants to know. And when they've done with you, get that fence finished and come back here. I'm off home to get into working clothes, but I'll soon be back.'

Pollard took an encouraging line.

'Come on, Bill. You lead the way up, but don't go too fast. We're twice your age, and Londoners into the bargain.'

The boy grinned broadly and headed in the direction of the woods. Behind the courtyard and the old stables at the back of Fairlynch Manor the hillside rose sharply. They passed under some great beeches just breaking into fragile green leaf, tramping over a thick carpet of last year's red-gold leaves. At intervals a stony track was visible, rising steeply and often disappearing under further drifts of dead leaves and conifer needles. Pollard and Toye scrutinised the ground carefully, while realising the virtual impossibility of finding recognisable traces of anyone who had walked over it six days earlier. Bill Manley watched them with fascinated interest, his face bright pink from the exertion of the rapid climb. Finally the gradient eased. The track bore left through a group of silver birches, beyond which a small wooden shed came in sight. It was very quiet. In the silence and sense of remoteness Pollard had an odd feeling of contact with the man who had come this way furtively and urgently in the dead hours of the previous Sunday morning, hurrying over the moonlit ground flecked with shadows to jettison his burden... Determination suddenly possessed him. Damn it all, the chap had come this way and was solid flesh and therefore traceable...

He realised that Bill Manley was staring at him.

'Tell us exactly what you did up here this morning, old man,' he said encouragingly.

Helped out by a few questions the boy

gave a clear account of his doings. He had been sent up to mend the fence soon after nine. After taking a look at the damage, he had gone to the shed to fetch a coil of wire. No, he hadn't gone right in, just opened the door and stretched out his hand for the wire which was hanging on a nail. He had got on well with the job, and about quarter past ten felt he'd earned a break and a fag. This time he had gone right inside the shed to get out of the wind for lighting up, and it was then that he had seen the black polythene bag in the dark corner by the door, and given it a kick, not meaning any harm.

'That's O.K.,' Pollard told him. 'I should probably have done the same myself. Can you see the Manor Farm buildings from up here?'

'Bit further along you can,' Bill Manley replied, and led the way to the spot where a fallen branch had been pulled clear of the partly repaired fence. A spade, a wooden mallet and lengths of wire were lying around, but Pollard's attention was instantly caught by the stile.

'Do many people come this way?' he asked.

Bill Manley's confusion spoke for itself, and Pollard grinned.

'I suppose you meet up with your girl-friend here in working hours? Does she come up from the farm?'

'Thassright,' the boy admitted. 'Susie Hayes, she's my girl. It ain't often we meets 'ere: jus' in an' out, school 'oliday times mostly, when she's 'ome.'

'Do people use the stile as a short cut between Manor Farm and Spireford village?'

'I ain't never seen none. 'Twould be trespassing on the Manor grounds, see?'

Pollard reflected that anyone who had explored the woods would know of the stile's existence. With Toye he examined it carefully, but they failed to find any signs of its having been crossed recently, either on the steps or on the ground on either side.

'Well, that's about the length of it,' he said at last as he straightened up. 'Thanks for your help, Bill. You'd better carry on with the fence or you'll have Mr Basing after you. Here's something to buy Susie a Coke next time you go out. We're just going to have a look at the shed, and then we'll be off.'

Conscious of being barely out of earshot, they talked in low voices as they stood in front of the small wooden building.

'No need for the chap to have gone inside,' Toye said. 'He'd only got to open the door by flipping up the hook, and chuck the bag into the corner.'

Pollard agreed, but they examined the floor closely with the help of a torch. The concrete surface had a thin covering of dust and earth. This had been recently trodden, but the prints were too confused for any to be clearly discernible.

'Well, one thing X didn't do was to spend the rest of Saturday night here,' Pollard said, after a further exhaustive search. 'At any rate we can be reasonably sure of that. Let's go down. I hate muttering like this.'

With a parting wave to Bill Manley, who was tackling the repair of the fence in a half-hearted way with an eye on the shed, they went down the path and round the Manor to their car.

Pollard looked at his watch.

'All this is taking up a lot of time, but I think we must go along to the farm. We can scout round at the road junction and see if there's anywhere handy where a get-away car could have been hidden. We can ask questions about barking dogs or whatever in the middle of Saturday night, and sounds of a car engine starting up. And we can also size up Hayes. He's nicely situated for the job, you know. Has he got it in for Heritage of Britain? Perhaps he wants to buy the farm and they won't play. There may not have been a car on the job at all. There are several pointers to X being a local, don't you think?'

'Meaning detailed knowledge of the layout of the Manor and the grounds?' Toye asked.

'Yes, and of what was in the exhibition.'

Toye sat in silent consideration of these ideas.

'Come to that,' he said at last, 'the Gilmores are local people, and so's the artist chap Rossiter. He lives near, doesn't he, in an old mill or something.'

'But all that lot were at the party on Saturday night, so they couldn't have hidden in the house during the afternoon when it was open. Gilmore's return from dropping Peck here within minutes of dropping Alix at the lodge is vouched for by Mrs Ridley and Alix herself, and Mrs Gilmore says her husband was back at home by eleven. Rossiter is an artist of some standing, and the idea of his trying to steal anything as difficult to dispose of as the Ridley portrait just doesn't make sense to me. It isn't even as though it's the sort of masterpiece that he might want to gloat over in secret. On paper Hayes is a much better candidate. Let's go along and

184

look at him.'

They turned right at the drive entrance, along the road running north from Spireford. On their right was the wall enclosing the main Fairlynch gardens, and on the left was the walled and detached water garden. Just beyond this they came to a white gate which was propped open by a large stone. It carried a board inscribed 'The Old Mill'. A rough unsurfaced road ran alongside a hedge, past the remains of a haystack under a tarpaulin, in the direction of a small group of buildings by the river. Toye was critical as he drove on.

'Shake the guts out of any car rattling it over a surface like that day in and day out,' he commented. 'You'd think a well-known artist could run to a bit of asphalt.'

'He probably never thinks of it,' Pollard replied. 'Easy. We're coming up to the farm turning.'

They prospected. The road to Manor Farm had been surfaced. It had open fields on either side, and ran dead straight between wire fences to the farm buildings. It offered no cover whatever to a waiting vehicle. The main road for some distance on either side had neither gateways nor side turnings where a car could have been concealed.

'Not conclusive, of course, but definitely not suited for lurking inconspicuously to pick a chap up,' Pollard said, as Toye turned and headed back in the direction of Manor Farm, agreeing reluctantly. It was obviously a going concern. Modern buildings in good repair flanked a solid stone-built house approached through a small flower garden full of daffodils and wallflowers. A continuous bass rumble of mooing came from the cowyard which was a shifting sea of black and white.

'Milking,' Pollard said. 'We shan't be popular.'

As he got out of the car, however, a short stocky man in a white overall emerged from the milking shed and came purposefully towards him. Shrewd eyes in a weather-beaten face summed him up.

'Mr Hayes? I'm sorry to come at an awkward time.'

'Hayes is the name. I reckon you'll be from Scotland Yard about the trouble up at the Manor. I can't tell you any more than I told the constable from Wellchester.'

'All the same, it's a help to get things at first hand, Mr Hayes. We won't keep you long.'

'Maybe we'd better step inside, then. I've

186

got a bit of an office for all the paperwork the government puts on us these days.'

A small but efficient office had been partitioned off in a building used for the storage of feedstuffs. The three men fitted in with some difficulty, and Pollard responded to Mr Hayes' brisk approach with equal conciseness. In a few minutes he had learnt that the farmer had been up until four o'clock on Sunday morning with a calving cow in difficulties. Mr Howlett, a vet from Wellchester, had been summoned by telephone and arrived soon after eleven on Saturday evening. He had stayed until three, when they reckoned the cow had pulled through and the calf was O.K. Mrs Hayes had been up all the time, providing hot drinks and snacks and anything else that was wanted. The dogs had been around, a bit bothered by all the fuss, and they'd have raised hell if they'd heard anyone coming down from the top, or a car starting up at the end of the road.

Pollard recognised conclusive evidence, even if Mr Howlett of Wellchester would have to be contacted for confirmation as a routine measure. He brought the conversation round to the tragedy at Fairlynch. Mr Hayes suddenly became human on the subject of the Ridley family and Francis Peck.

'It seemed like the end of the world to us the day Mr Ridley told me he was making over the estate to Heritage of Britain. But if you'd searched the country from north to south you couldn't've found a nicer chap than poor Mr Peck. Knew his job, and knew I knows mine, an' we got on like a house afire. Now he's gone, and what we'll get in his place, God only knows,' he concluded gloomily.

'Well, that's the end of the Hayes lead all right,' Pollard said as they drove along the farm road. 'He couldn't have done it on grounds of practical possibility, or on psychological grounds either if I know anything at all about human nature. I can't wait to get back to Wellchester, but I think there's one more job we'd better get done first which ties up with this dumping of the pictures.'

'Mrs Ridley and the girl?' Toye asked.

'Yes. I'd like to question them myself about possible footsteps past the lodge in the middle of Saturday night, or a car starting up. Mrs R has obviously been mixed up in funny business of some sort, you know.'

A transformed Katharine Ridley opened the door of the lodge, relaxed, confident and full of vitality. In a flash Pollard realised that she

188

had simply reverted to her normal self. The question which immediately formed in his mind was answered by the copy of *The Monitor* on the sitting room table, open at the page carrying the report of the fatal road accident near Brynsworthy. As he exchanged civilities he wondered what she had been blackmailed about by the man in the duffle coat.

'Do sit down,' she was saying. 'Alix will be back any time now for her tea. Can I give you both a cup?'

Pollard declined politely.

'There's been a surprising development, Mrs Ridley,' he told her, watching her closely as he spoke. 'Some, if not all of the pictures that were stolen on Saturday night have been found.'

Her reaction was to stare at him blankly for a second, as if trying to get this information into context. Then astonishment came into her face.

'But how splendid!' she exclaimed. 'Did you and Inspector Toye find them? Where are they?'

'I'm afraid we can't claim any of the credit,' Pollard replied. 'They were found by one of the under-gardeners, Bill Manley, when he went up to mend the fence at the top of the woods this morning. They were in a black polythene bag in the shed up there.'

'But what on earth was the point of taking the pictures and then leaving them practically on the doorstep?'

'That's one of the things we want to find out. Another is where the thief went afterwards. After making enquiries we're satisfied that it's very unlikely that he went down to Manor Farm and out to the main road that way. An alternative escape route would be to return on his tracks, and come down the drive past this house. I know both you and Miss Parr have already told Inspector Rendell that you didn't hear anything unusual during the night, but I want you to go over the ground again, and see if anything however small comes to your minds. You were unwell, weren't you? Did you have a wakeful night?'

Pollard got the impression that the reference to her being unwell was uncongenial. She quickly shut her eyes as if to help her to concentrate.

'No,' she said, opening them again. 'I slept like a log. Alix gave me hot milk and whisky before she went out, and I took two aspirins. I was soon drowsy, and heard the Gilmore car come back and drop her, and didn't rouse myself to talk when she came into my room. She went away again, and I heard the car coming back and turning out into the road. The next thing was waking up and hearing Tom Basing hammering on the door... Here's Alix.'

The front door opened and closed again.

'We're back,' a young voice called, and Terry erupted into the sitting room. On catching sight of Pollard and Toye he stopped dead, a front paw raised clear of the ground and ears pricked.

'Friends, Terry,' Katharine told him firmly. 'As long as people are with us he's satisfied. It was finding you on your own in the house that set him off the other day, Inspector Toye... Alix, here's Superintendent Pollard.'

Alix came to the door, slightly dishevelled and muddy.

'Hallo!' she said, smiling at him. 'I'd better just take these shoes off before I come in. We had a colossal walk, Gran. I think I've worn Terry out.'

The terrier slumped into his basket, re-assured but keeping a watchful eye on Pollard and Toye. Alix reappeared and sank on to a chair, and Pollard reported the finding of the missing pictures once again.

'How absolutely super!' she exclaimed. 'Is

one of them the thing of the Spire that Lydia Gilmore bought? I do hope so.'

Pollard explained that he had not yet examined the pictures because they had to be gone over for fingerprints before being handled any more.

'But it's simply bonkers, though, isn't it? I mean, why bother to take them if you were going to dump them again almost at once?'

Pollard replied in the same terms as he had to the identical comment from Katharine Ridley, and again brought the conversation round to the events of Saturday evening.

'Try to remember every little detail from the time when the party at Mr and Mrs Gilmore's broke up,' he said. 'You see, it looks as though an escape car may have been parked somewhere near here. Did you happen to notice a car in a gateway, for instance, as you were driven back?'

To his relief this improbable suggestion passed muster without question.

'I'm sure there wasn't,' Alix said. 'At least, I couldn't absolutely swear to it, I suppose, as we were talking, but I'd have noticed, I think. Have you asked Hugo Rossiter? He'd gone on ahead.'

'Was he much ahead of you?' Pollard asked.

'Oh, no. Lydia wanted to send Gran some

food that would come in for Professor Chilmark's lunch the next day, so there wouldn't be so much to do, as she – Gran, I mean – wasn't feeling well. So we took a few minutes longer to stow them in the boot with a bottle of champagne to zip Gran up. Malcolm dashed down to the cellar for it, and then we started off. They're both awfully generous.'

On arrival at the lodge Francis Peck had helped transport the food and champagne to the door of the lodge, and seen Alix into the house. She described 'shushing' Terry who had been waiting on the mat, and who showed a disposition to bark with excitement at her return. Then she had tiptoed into her grandmother's room, found her asleep and crept out again.

'You told Inspector Rendell that you heard Mr Gilmore's car come back from the Manor after dropping Mr Peck, I think. You're quite sure it was Mr Gilmore returning, and not some other car?'

Here Alix was definite. She knew the sound of the Gilmore car, and it had come back very soon. She had hardly stowed away the food and started going to bed when it went past.

'Besides, if the car I heard was another

one, I'd have heard Malcolm's too,' she argued. 'I'm sure I didn't hear two.'

Asked about any sounds of a passing car, footsteps or Terry barking during the night, she shook her head emphatically.

'I was flat out. It was late and I'd had a few drinks, actually,' she added a shade self-consciously. 'The first thing I heard was poor old Tom Basing at the door next morning. And it was an awfully windy night. The wind was making a terrific noise in the drive trees, and I remember wedging my window before I got into bed.'

Feeling that there was nothing more to be learnt from Katharine Ridley or Alix at the moment, Pollard thanked them both for their help, and asked when it was planned to reopen the gardens and 'Pictures for Pleasure'.

'On Monday, all going well,' she told him. 'Heritage of Britain are sending someone down to act as temporary Warden. He's going to live at the pub until poor Hilary is ready to move out. Mr Rossiter is up at the Manor at the moment, getting "Pictures for Pleasure" straight. He did the actual hanging, you know. I'm going along to lend a hand presently.'

'It would be a saving of time if we went up

for a word with him now,' Pollard said. 'We'll go at once. Perhaps you wouldn't mind waiting for a short time before you come along?'

'Not in the least,' she assured him. 'We haven't had our tea yet.'

The two cars that they had noticed before were still parked on the terrace outside the Manor. To avoid disturbing the Pecks in their meeting with Heritage of Britain representatives, they walked round to the windows of the library and looked in. A man in light-coloured slacks and an open-necked shirt was scrutinising the picture he was holding. He glanced up, made a gesture of recognition and came to the window.

'I'll let you in at the front,' he called to them.

As they arrived on the terrace a key turned in a lock, and a tall well-built man with crisp black hair and strong, rather heavy features eyed them shrewdly.

'I'm Rossiter,' he said. 'You're the Yard, I take it? Come in. I'm trying to pick up the pieces.'

'Thanks,' Pollard said, as they followed him across the hall and down the short passage to the library. He saw that the Ridley portrait had been re-hung. A number of smaller pictures were scattered about, propped on chairs and lying on a small table inside the door.

'Finding possible paintings of the right size to fill the gaps is like doing a bloody jigsaw,' Hugo Rossiter commented, clearing some chairs. 'Take a pew, won't you? I don't know that I can be much help to you.'

'Perhaps you've heard that anyway some of the stolen pictures were found this morning, Mr Rossiter?' Pollard asked.

'Good God, man! Where? Can we have 'em back in time for reopening on Monday?'

'I'm afraid not, until the enquiry is finished. They're being tested for fingerprints at the moment.'

'You'll find 'em smothered in mine. I did most of the hanging.'

'We realise that, and one reason for coming along to see you is to ask for a set of your prints to help the dabs experts.'

'Sure. Go ahead. When and where did the pictures turn up?'

While Toye went into action Pollard once again gave an account of Bill Manley's discovery.

'I can't tell you if all five have turned up,'

he concluded. 'Naturally I didn't investigate the contents of the bag before they were tested by the dabs chaps at Wellchester.'

'The only one worth recovering is the Boyd-Calthrop "Head of an Old Peasant",' Hugo Rossiter replied emphatically. 'Extraordinary business, isn't it? Sheer lunacy from start to finish, with a perfectly ghastly outcome which I'm certain was never intended.'

'What is your personal interpretation of the whole affair, Mr Rossiter?' Pollard asked.

'As I've just said: sheer lunacy. It isn't an art robbery in the real sense of the word. No one with even a minimal knowledge of art would set out to steal this not particularly good and quite unsaleable portrait' – he indicated 'The Young Heir' – 'and still less would a sane person try to pull off the job up here where there's at least basic security. Perfectly simple to break into the lodge when Mrs Ridley was away. And it equally obviously isn't a homicide. How could whoever did it have known that a north wind would make that bloody boiler house a death trap?' he asked bitterly.

'Whoever it was managed somehow to get hold of a key to this room,' Pollard said.

Hugo Rossiter stretched out his legs in

front of him and thrust his hands into his trouser pockets in a relaxed manner.

'Francis Peck was a careful type,' he said, 'but nobody's infallible. After the exhibits started coming in he locked the door, and put the key on his key ring with his ignition and safe keys, so what? Did the poor chap never leave his ignition key in the car when it was standing on the terrace out there? We're all human. He could have heard the telephone ringing, for instance and dashed into the house. Or let me offer another line of enquiry. Who fitted the mortice lock in the first place, in John Ridley's day? Was there originally a third key?'

'Your first suggestion supports the strong probability that someone local is involved,' Pollard remarked.

'I couldn't agree more.' Hugo Rossiter raised his eyebrows interrogatively and grinned with a touch of mockery. 'Any hopes you have of trapping me into a confession are misplaced.'

Pollard declined the bait.

'Do you know of anyone locally who has a grudge – real or imaginary – against Mrs Ridley? Or had one against Mr Peck as representing Heritage of Britain?'

'I'm as certain as one can be that I should

have heard of anything of the sort, and I never have. I drop in at the pub several times a week, and my business in Wellchester brings me into touch with a lot of people round here. You've thought of rabid anti-conservationists, I expect, who might have it in for HOB?... Here's Katharine Ridley. She's come up to help sort things out for re-opening on Monday...' He broke off to acknowledge her arrival outside the window, and indicate the direction of the front door. 'Is there anything more I can tell you?'

'Did you notice any car on the road, or one parked alongside on your way back from the party on Saturday night?'

'No. I can be quite definite about that. I remember thinking that it was unusual for a Saturday night. I'd left while the others were still stowing some food for the lodge into the boot of Malcolm Gilmore's car, and it hadn't caught me up by the time I turned into my gate.'

'Did you by any chance hear a car on the road later in the night? After twelve, say?'

'If I did, I've no recollection of it. As soon as I got in, I settled down to work on an article for an art journal, a job that involved the hell of a lot of concentration. I didn't get it finished and typed out until nearly one, and then turned in. I'm a fair way off the road, you know, and it was blowing quite hard into the bargain.'

'Well, thanks very much for your help,' Pollard said, getting to his feet. 'We'll notify both you and Mrs Ridley when we know which of the missing pictures have been found, and also their owners. And they'll be kept under suitable conditions, of course.'

Katharine Ridley and Alix were waiting at the front door, and after a few minutes' conversation went into the house with Hugo Rossiter, while Pollard and Toye got into their car.

'That chap's no fool,' Pollard remarked. 'That's what makes me feel we can count him out, although we've no evidence that he drove straight home and stayed there: simply his word for it.'

'You mean he might have driven to the Manor ahead of Gilmore, and gone in with Peck, saying he wanted to do some job in the exhibition?' Toye asked; letting in the clutch.

'Yes, but take it a stage further. Can you imagine him suddenly knocking Peck out, trussing him up and locking him in the boiler house, not to mention mucking about with the Ridley portrait and the other pictures? It

200

would have been a bit awkward the next morning when Peck returned to the scene, wouldn't it? No, whatever the answer is, it isn't that.'

As the car approached the lodge, frenzied barking was audible.

'Your four-legged pal again,' Pollard said. 'Would you – hold it!'

Toye braked sharply. A young man who was peering through the sitting room window swung round defensively. Pollard registered under-average height, a tendency to overweight straining a grey suit, full cheeks, red hair, and spectacles in pale frames.

'Are you looking for Mrs Ridley?' he enquired coolly.

'I've come to see Alix Parr.' The accent was slightly flat and nasal.

'Miss Parr is not in,' Pollard informed him, 'and won't be for some time.'

The young man gave him a resentful look, muttered something about it not being worth waiting, and headed for the drive entrance and the road.

Following slowly in the Rover, Pollard and Toye watched him get into a Mini parked close to the hedge. He ignored them pointedly as they drove past. In their driving mirrors they watched him turning the car, presumably to follow them in the direction of Wellchester.

'Reckon she can do better than that,' Toye remarked.

Chapter 8

During the drive back to Wellchester it was settled that while Pollard conferred with the fingerprint and photographic experts, Toye could check Mr Hayes's alibi for the previous Saturday night with Mr Howlett, the veterinary surgeon.

'And you can go on from him to call on some of the people whose pictures have turned up,' Pollard said. 'The Allbrights and a Mr and Mrs Coote live in Wellchester. Watch their reactions, and see if you can get on to anything, especially the arty Allbrights. I've been wondering what we'd better work on next if we draw a blank over the dabs. My idea is to call on Lady Boyd-Calthrop early tomorrow, and get her going on local history. I only hope old Chilmark's right about her being a mine of information on the subject. I'll give her a ring and try to fix a time. Then I'm sure we ought to see if it's possible to get any confirmation of two people's unsupported statements: Rossiter's and Basing's.'

'Meaning that there was no witness to

Basing finding the body?' Toye asked.

'That's one thing. And at the moment we've simply his word for it that he went home on Saturday evening after paying in his money from the sale of plants to Francis Peck. In theory he could have hidden in the Manor. And by the way, up to now we've simply accepted from him that the Fairlynch car park was empty by about 5.45 pm. We may come back to your idea about a getaway car being left there after all. I wonder if the local chaps have managed to get on to George Palmer's trail yet? If they've had any luck, that would give us another line to work on. After all, he was obviously blackmailing the ex-Lady of the Manor, and it seems quite on the cards that he was the bloke thrown out for doing an unauthorised tour of the house.'

They discussed possible programmes for the next day, Pollard admitting that he was not hopeful of getting fresh information from Bill Manley's find. Within half an hour of returning to the police station he was proved right. The Wellchester technicians had worked enthusiastically on the polythene bag and its contents, enjoying the opportunity of co-operating with a famous Yard Super, but from the standpoint of establishing the thief's identity nothing had been achieved. All five paintings had been in the bag, and all had been extensively handled by Hugo Rossiter, obviously during their hanging for 'Pictures for Pleasure'. Superimposed on his prints were others made by some wearing rubber gloves. These were identical with the prints found in the library, and on the boiler house and side doors of the Manor. Over these again were those made by Bill Manley during his inspection of the bag's contents. Prints on the polythene bag itself were exclusively the rubber glove variety and Bill Manley's. Of Tom Basing's there was not a single trace.

The Wellchester fingerprint and photography experts were crestfallen. Pollard assured them that their labours had not been in vain.

'At any rate,' he said, 'I think we can take it that the chap who did the job in Fairlynch Manor was the same one who dumped this little lot in the shed.'

The photographer scratched his ginger head in bewilderment.

'Reckon the bloke was barmy, sir,' he commented.

'It certainly looks like it at the moment,' Pollard agreed. 'All the same, when we get to the end of the road I shan't be surprised to find that there was method in his madness. I expect I shall be coming back on you boys for some more help soon.'

They went off cheered at this prospect, and he decided to examine the pictures in case they provided some unexpected clue, either collectively or individually. He extracted Inspector Rendell's notes from the file, and propped the five paintings on convenient ledges and chairs. Collectively all that they appeared to have in common was modest size, making them a manageable load. They were, in fact, a very varied assortment. Thanks to his art education by Jane, Pollard could see the technical weaknesses in Lady Boyd-Calthrop's 'Head of an Old Peasant' that Professor Chilmark had mentioned. But the wrinkled weather-beaten face with its knowing eyes was likeable and convincing. One could live with it. Next to it on the mantelpiece was 'Inspiration', an oil by Ann Bilton of the Wellchester Art Club, for which Lydia Gilmore had astonishingly paid £25. Pollard gazed at it in bewilderment. Running vertically down the dead centre of the picture was an irregular zigzag of dirty grey. It ricocheted from side to side of a vivid emerald green trough, gnawing at steep rocky slopes. Finally he decided that the painting could symbolise the evolution of the Spire Valley down the millennia, and probably quite a lot in the artist's subconscious. With a shudder at the bright scarlet frame, he moved on to 'Oleanders on Lake Lugano'. The glass of this watercolour's frame was broken, so it was probably the picture hung below the Ridley portrait which seemed to have been knocked down or dropped, the noise of its fall possibly bringing Francis Peck downstairs. Unlike 'Inspiration' it was purely representational. Grey-green oleander trees on the lakeside were in full pink bloom. There was no focal point and no statement about anything. According to Inspector Rendell's notes it was the work of Henri Legrand and the property of Mr and Mrs Coote of Wellchester, who had valued it modestly at £5. Pollard turned it over. It was inscribed on the back 'Our Honeymoon. Jim and Joy'.

I'm becoming an art snob, he thought, and picked up Malcolm Gilmore's 'Flight into Egypt', described in the notes as 'oil painting, 12 x 6 inches, after Lecci, by Alfred Gilmore, great-uncle of the owner. Family interest only: of no monetary value'. Dull browns and greens predominated, and a ruined castle, a lake and a small boat distracted attention from the Holy Family's precipitate flight from Herod. Putting the little painting down again, Pollard turned with relief to the last of the five, and decided at once that he would like to own it. This one, 'Frosty Morning', was also an oil but full of light. Snowdrops in a glass bowl on a window sill echoed the whiteness of rimed grass and plants seen through a misty window. Rex Allbright, the owner, valued the painting by someone called L. G. Hanford (1910) at £350. Pollard made a mental note to ask Jane about L. G. Hanford, and then, feeling guilty at having spent time on art criticism instead of pure detection, he collected the paintings and took them back to Inspector Rendell's office for safe keeping.

On returning to his room he put through a telephone call to Weatherwise Farm. It was answered by Lydia Gilmore.

'Superintendent Pollard here, Mrs Gilmore,' he said. 'I'm ringing to let you and your husband know that both your exhibits in "Pictures for Pleasure" have been recovered undamaged.'

She exclaimed in surprise, and asked the inevitable question about where and when they had been found.

'Fantastic!' she reacted on hearing the details. 'Honestly, this business gets crazier every day! What *can* it all add up to?'

Pollard replied that the lead given by the recovery of the pictures was being followed up, and that in the meantime the paintings were perfectly safe and being kept under suitable conditions until they could be returned.

'Oh, we shan't lose any sleep over what's happening to them,' Lydia told him breezily. 'I only bought "Inspiration" on a public-spirited impulse to encourage local talent, and that pathetic effort of Malcolm's great-uncle just takes up space on the wall. Our children are simply ribald about it. Has Lady Boyd-Calthrop's "Head of an Old Peasant" turned up too? She's so fond of it.'

Pollard reassured her on this point and shortly afterwards brought the call to an end. He then rang Lady Boyd-Calthrop at the Dower House of Firle. A harsh confident voice informed him that she was speaking.

'Good morning,' he said. 'This is Detective Chief Superintendent Pollard of New Scotland Yard. You may, perhaps, have heard that I am conducting the enquiry into the late Mr Francis Peck's death?'

'Of course I have, my dear man,' the voice replied, now less abrasive. 'It's the talk of the neighbourhood. How do I come in, may I ask?'

'In the first place as an exhibitor in "Pictures for Pleasure", Lady Boyd-Calthrop,' Pollard told her. 'Your "Head of an Old Peasant" has been recovered unharmed and is being kept at Wellchester police station. It will be returned to you at the end of the enquiry. It was found this morning with the other four missing pictures in the shed at the top of the Fairlynch woods.'

He waited for a surprised exclamation but none came. There was a pause.

'Obviously whoever put them there meant them to be found,' Lady Boyd-Calthrop commented decisively. 'It's useless to ask you what you make of it, I suppose?'

'At the moment, yes,' Pollard replied with equal directness. 'My second reason for making this call is to ask if I may call on you tomorrow morning. Not particularly in connection with these paintings, but I think you might be able to help me in other directions.'

'Call by all means,' she replied. 'It seems most unlikely to me that I can, but I shall be most interested to see you. At what time may I expect you?'

An appointment was made for ten o'clock, and after giving explicit directions for finding the Dower House, Lady Boyd-Calthrop rang off. As Pollard put down the receiver Toye came into the room.

'Well? Any luck?' Pollard asked, throwing himself back in his chair and clasping his hands behind his head.

'All of 'em were in,' Toye reported, sitting down at the opposite side of the table, 'and that's a bit of luck for a Friday evening, I suppose. I took Mr Howlett first, thinking he'd be having a surgery, and so he was. And a cut above our doctors' place at home the waiting room was, I can tell you. Beautiful pot plants and a tank of fish. Howlett is an earnest young chap who's just been taken on as a partner, and he's careful and accurate in what he says. The call from Hayes came through just after eleven last Saturday night, and he went straight off in his car as soon as he'd got what was wanted, getting to Manor Farm at about twenty to twelve, and left again at ten minutes past three. The only bonus point is that as he'd never been to the farm before and it was dark, he hesitated a bit as he got near, and stopped at the gate of Mr Rossiter's place to read the name on it. He says he didn't see any car parked inside, only the remains of a haystack and some farm machinery with a tarpaulin over it, but he noticed a light in a building across the field.'

'Possibly useful, but not conclusive, of course,' Pollard commented. 'Rossiter could have got a time clock gadget to switch a light on. What else?'

'Nothing more from Howlett, except that he didn't meet or see any car on the Spireford road, either coming or going. I went on to the Cootes next. They're a pleasant ordinary couple in their fifties, I'd say, and pleased as a pair of kids when I told them their picture had turned up. Seems they bought it on their honeymoon as a souvenir. They've got an alibi for the whole of Saturday and Sunday: daughter, son-in-law and baby staying the weekend. I took the name and address, saying it was routine.'

'What about Allbright, the President of the Wellchester Art Club?'

'The Allbrights are a cut above the Cootes. They've a bigger house in a more classy suburb. He's a Bank manager. The place was full of pictures, and they both seem to know a lot about them, and were thrilled to bits that their missing one had been found. He said the insurance money wouldn't have been the same thing at all. They've got alibis, too. They stayed until after "Pictures for Pleasure" closed on Saturday, and helped tidy things up. Mr Allbright remembered seeing Basing in the hall just before they left, and made a joking sort of remark about him being dead against the exhibition from the word go. The Allbrights are gardeners and buy plants from him, they say. They left just on six, and gave a couple of friends a lift back to Wellchester and asked them in to supper. I got their names and addresses, too.'

Pollard stretched and yawned.

'Well, we didn't expect much from this lot, did we? I rang Mrs Gilmore, who seemed moderately pleased that their two pictures had turned up, and I've got an appointment with Lady Boyd-Calthorp for tea tomorrow... Come in!'

A constable entered and saluted smartly.

'Superintendent Maynard's compliments, sir, and he'd be glad if you could spare him a few minutes.'

'Thanks,' Pollard said. 'We'll be right along.'

They found the Superintendent in a state of imperfectly concealed gratification. His men had picked up the trail of George Palmer in two different places. On the strength of his visit to Fairlynch a call had been made at the Wellchester Information Centre. A woman who had been in charge there on the previous Saturday morning was shown the description of Palmer and his photograph, and had identified him without hesitation as the man who had called at the Centre at about midday, saying that he was on holiday in the area and wanted to know of any places of interest to visit. She had given him pamphlets about various houses and gardens open to the public, including one on Fairlynch.

'Here's a copy of it,' Superintendent Maynard said, passing it over to Pollard. 'Then my chaps interviewed the conductors of all the late morning and early afternoon buses going both to Spireford village and past the Spireford turning on the road to Brynscombe. The conductor of the 2.20 pm from Wellchester say he can remember a bloke in a fawn duffel coat getting off at the turning, which the bus is scheduled to reach at 2.45 pm. And as you'll see from the Ordnance map there's a footpath along the river. The bloke could have bypassed the village by following this, if he was up to something shady, and cut up on to the road just beyond Fairlynch. That would explain him not being noticed in the village. And the timing seems reasonable for doing the walk and arriving at the ticket office round a quarter past three. We've had no luck about how he got back to

Wellchester, but there is a bus from Bryns-combe which passes the turning at 5.30 pm, and he could have gone back by the footpath, I suppose, and got in here at five to six. Plenty of time to get some grub and prospect round before pinching the first car.'

Pollard and Toye agreed that this reconstruction of Palmer's movements held water, and offered tactful congratulations on the results achieved by the Wellchester force.

'All right as far as it goes,' Superintendent Maynard replied, 'but what we want is evidence of some contact Palmer made, since he couldn't have done the Fairlynch job himself. However, we'll press on.'

In the corridor outside Pollard and Toye exchanged glances.

'Basing?' Toye queried.

'Could be, I suppose,' Pollard replied.

'One of tomorrow's jobs will be trying to find out if he's got an alibi for Saturday evening and night. We'll go out to Spireford as soon as I'm through with her ladyship.'

The Boyd-Calthrop Dower House was on the outskirts of the village of Clearwell St Philip, two miles from Firle, the family's Palladian mansion in its extensive park. Pollard had expected something more impressive, and was surprised at being directed by a local inhabitant merely to one of the large village houses. However, it was, he recognised, very pleasing – two-storied and of grey stone, with mullioned windows. A short drive through a garden full of spring colour brought him to the front door. He got out of his car, glanced round with appreciation and rang the bell. A comfortable-looking country woman in a nylon overall answered the door.

'That's right,' she said, inspecting the official card he presented to her. 'Her ladyship's expecting you. Please to step this way.'

He was shown into a panelled sitting room overlooking the garden. An elderly woman with white hair cut short, strong features and sharp dark eyes held out her hand.

'Forgive my not getting up,' she said. 'I'm a bit seized up with the rheumatics this morning. Just Anno Domini, you know... So you're the Scotland Yard celebrity they've sent us? Well, well, I never expected to welcome a famous detective to my house. Take that chair where I can have a good look at you.'

Pollard complied. As they talked about 'Head of an Old Peasant' and its recovery he was aware of being keenly eyed.

'Well, young man,' Lady Boyd-Calthrop

suddenly said, abruptly changing the conversation, 'I've all the time in the world at my age, but presumably you haven't. What have you really come to see me about?'

'To get some local colour,' he replied unequivocally with a smile. A brief cackle reassured him: he had taken the right line.

'As I thought,' she commented. 'We'll talk better over a cup of tea, though. It's never too early for a midmorning cup. Would you kindly touch the bell over there by the fireplace?'

Pollard rose and walked across the room, feeling, as he afterwards told Jane, that he had stepped back into the Edwardian era. Before he had got back to his chair, the woman who had let him in appeared.

'Tea, Annie, please,' Lady Boyd-Calthrop requested. 'Connoisseur's Lapsang Souchong or a good sound Darjeeling, Superintendent Pollard?'

He asked for Darjeeling and got an approving nod.

'Good man. I like tea to taste of tea, not of scent. The Darjeeling then, Annie. Now then,' she went on as the door closed, 'I'm at your disposal.'

Pollard decided against any attempt at finesse.

'The Fairlynch case is an extremely odd one,' he said. 'May I take it that you are familiar with the main facts?'

'You may. I have absorbed every line on it in the local and reputable national newspapers.'

'In that case I think you will probably agree with me, Lady Boyd-Calthrop, that it's a curiously unconvincing affair. Please don't think for a moment that we are taking Mr Peck's death lightly. However, I am certain that it was never part of the original plan. And as things have turned out, I'm far from convinced that there was ever any intention to steal pictures either. Could the whole business have been planned as a practical joke or a spiteful gesture against Mrs Ridley or Heritage of Britain? This is what I want to discuss with you. I feel that you must be well up in local politics.'

He got a shrewd glance.

'You are satisfied that someone local was responsible?'

'I think it's possible that more than one person was involved although I have no proof of this at present. But the evidence points to a detailed knowledge of the Manor and its grounds, and of the arrangements for "Pictures for Pleasure" on somebody's part. There is also the matter of access to a key to the library.'

Lady Boyd-Calthrop nodded decisively.

'I agree. And there is also the matter of Hilary Peck's absence on Saturday night which could not have been very widely known, surely?'

'That has occurred to us, too. But on enquiry it seems impossible to discover with any accuracy who the people were who knew that she would be away that night.'

'Quite.'

The conversation was momentarily held up by the arrival of the tea trolley. There was a pause while Lady Boyd-Calthrop occupied herself in pouring out. When she spoke again her comments were unexpected.

'In my view,' she said, 'a practical joke as objectionable as this one could hardly be distinguished from a spiteful gesture. I take it that what you are asking me is whether I know of anyone in the neighbourhood who would have behaved in this way towards Mrs Ridley or Heritage of Britain. The timing of the attack suggests to me that the target may have been "Pictures for Pleasure" rather than Heritage in general. Why anyone should have behaved in such a fashion is beyond my comprehension, but you know better than I the extraordinary things people do these days. The point I want to make is that although the exhibition was Katharine Ridley's idea in the first place, a great deal of the work has been done by Hugo Rossiter, and Francis Peck was involved too, of course, as the Fairlynch Warden. There is also Rex Allbright, who organised the Wellchester Art Club's part.'

Pollard listened with mounting respect for the old lady's acumen.

'Thank you,' he said. 'The idea of "Pictures for Pleasure" as a kind of catalyst causing an old grievance to erupt into action has begun to take shape in my own mind. As you point out, more people than Mrs Ridley were involved in putting on the show. May I have your views on the likelihood of any one of them being the real target of the attack?'

'You may,' Lady Boyd-Calthrop replied, after a pause during which she drank tea with relish from a Crown Derby cup. 'In my opinion, for what it is worth, Rex Allbright is a non-starter. He only became involved in "Pictures for Pleasure" because the Wellchester Art Club members were invited to exhibit, with the idea of filling up wall space and getting the free loan of the Club's

220

display screens. Do you agree?'

Pollard agreed that Rex Allbright could be disregarded as an intended victim.

'What about Mr Peck?' he asked.

'He had only been at Fairlynch since the autumn of '75, you know. We were all rather apprehensive about the sort of man Heritage would put in as Warden, and I can only say that Francis Peck was liked from the start. And respected. He knew his job and did it. As a person he was delightful: intelligent, sensitive and modest. Never a brash new broom although there was a great deal to be done. I can only say with absolute truth that I've never heard adverse criticism of him from any quarter.'

'From any quarter?' Pollard queried. 'That's a remarkably comprehensive testimonial. Employees are usually highly critical when there's a take-over.'

Lady Boyd-Calthrop gave another short cackle of laughter.

'Another cup of tea? I expect you've been treated to Tom Basing's views on "Pictures for Pleasure". I was myself a few weeks ago. But don't take them as criticism of Francis Peck for allowing the exhibition to be held, or of Katharine Ridley. According to Tom it was the grasping Heritage Council trying to make money out of Fairlynch. He worships Katharine in his forthright way. He's known her ever since she came here as a bride before the war, you see. And he and Francis Peck got on like a house on fire.'

Pollard accepted his second cup of tea, and brought the conversation round to Hugo Rossiter. He saw Lady Boyd-Calthrop's authoritative expression soften slightly.

'I've a soft spot for Hugo Rossiter in spite of his obvious failings,' she admitted. 'He's intelligent – I rate intelligence highly, Superintendent – and most amusing. A very gifted artist, of course, and rather surprisingly, a good business man. His art shop in Wellchester is highly profitable, I understand.'

'What are his obvious failings?' Pollard asked.

'Primarily selfishness, the result of talent and success. He's inclined to throw a commitment up if he gets bored, however inconvenient to other people. Katharine Ridley was in a panic that this would happen over "Pictures for Pleasure". There were tiresome delays and he seemed to be getting fretty. And frankly his moral life is not what I can approve of, although I will say that he is discreet about it.'

Pollard concealed his amusement at Lady

Boyd-Calthrop's order of priority over Hugo Rossiter's failings.

'Isn't it rather surprising that an artist of Mr Rossiter's standing should have given so much time to a modest affair like "Pictures for Pleasure"?'

'I was a little surprised myself. But he is generous and kind-hearted on impulse, and fond of Katharine Ridley. He'll do a lot for his friends, provided that their demands don't become boring to him. And in a rather sardonic way he does a lot to encourage popular interest in art. "Pictures for Pleasure" would appeal to him on that score, you see.'

'He sounds to me the sort of man who might make enemies,' Pollard said cautiously, making a mental note to talk to Rex Allbright about the reactions of the local art circle to Hugo Rossiter.

'He does rile some people,' Lady Boyd-Calthrop admitted. 'The stuffier local members of what seems to be known as the Establishment these days. But I wouldn't say that he makes lasting enemies exactly. He'd get tired of keeping up a vendetta: his sense of humour would come to the rescue. But I can't think of a single person in this part of the world who would go to the length of doing what was done at Fairlynch to spite him, especially as Francis Peck and Katharine Ridley would suffer from it, too. I have heard rumours,' she went on after a brief pause, 'that he has brought off some coups over pictures which other dealers have looked askance at, but I don't know any details. Temperamentally he'd enjoy taking speculative risks.'

Pollard made a mental note of this information and moved on to another topic.

'We're interested in the final break-up of the party at Weatherwise Farm on the Saturday night,' he said. 'The timing is vital in our opinion. Would you say that Mr and Mrs Gilmore are likely to be time-conscious?'

Lady Boyd-Calthrop glanced at him in amusement.

'What you're really trying to get out of me is what I think of the Gilmores, isn't it? They're a popular hospitable couple, and I always enjoy an evening there. Mrs Gilmore is an able amusing woman and I shouldn't expect her to bother much about the time when she's entertaining. Her husband is a good host but I find him less congenial – rather given to airing his grievances against the government, which is so boring. And obviously his firm is doing very nicely, too.

I'm sure he's highly efficient in his office and organises his time to the minute, but I've never seen any sign of this at one of the Weatherwise parties.'

'Thank you,' Pollard said. 'Now I'd like to ask you about the Ridleys. Mr John Ridley died about two and a half years ago, I understand. Were he and his wife liked locally when they were living at the Manor?'

'Very much. This sounds dated, I know, but they were English landed gentry at its best: public-spirited, charitable and hospitable. And Katharine has been much admired for the way in which she accepted her husband's death and the good grace with which she stepped down. Here again, I cannot think of a single soul who would have wanted to injure something that she had worked hard to make a success. Not at the present time, that is. I wouldn't have put it past Alix's regrettable father if he had lived.'

With a quickening of interest which he could not explain Pollard asked if both Alix Parr's parents were dead.

'Yes, both of them,' Lady Boyd-Calthrop told him. She pushed the tea trolley aside, and leant back in her chair. 'It's a tragic story. Briefly the Ridleys made the fatal mistake of bringing up Helen – Alix's mother and their only child – for the pre-1939 world, not realising that it was going for good. The result was that when she came back from her finishing school abroad she simply kicked over the traces. She had a little money of her own, went off to London, and after various affairs fell madly in love with Geoffrey Parr. She brought him down here. I thought him absolutely beyond the pale: amoral, coolly calculating, and obviously thinking he was on to a good thing. You can imagine the dear static Ridleys' reaction. I gather that it was made abundantly clear that no settlement would be made on Helen if they married. The pair went back to London, married belatedly, Helen being pregnant, and left for Paris for some alleged job of Geoffrey Parr's. He deserted her almost at once. She was too proud to admit it to her parents, and struggled on under dreadful conditions, finally dying in childbirth. Two months before her death, Geoffrey Parr's body was found in the Seine.'

'What a ghastly story,' Pollard said with feeling, his mind assimilating the facts and reaching out to their possible relevance to the present. 'And Alix has been brought up by her grandparents. I suppose she's about eighteen now?'

'Eighteen in August. All this happened in 1960. The Ridleys hushed it up as far as they could, of course, but I'm a very old friend. The ironic part is that although they tried hard to avoid the same mistake over Alix, and have given her a comparatively democratic upbringing, she's showing unmistakeable signs of kicking over the traces in her turn, only in the opposite direction. The contemporary social conscience, you know. And the child's quite obviously in love with the nice but rather dull Kit Peck. He teaches in a slum school and didn't go to a public school himself, although he won a scholarship to Oxford. Poor Katharine is distraught. She's coming over to lunch with me today to pour out her troubles. She's just as static as ever, poor darling, without realising it for a moment... I'm afraid I haven't been very much help to you, have I?'

'On the contrary, you've done valuable filling-in for me,' Pollard assured her. 'It was only last Monday that I first heard of the people we've been talking about. I'm grateful to you.'

'I don't know that it'll get you much further,' Lady Boyd-Calthrop replied bluntly. 'However, I'm glad to have been of some little use. I simply cannot stomach Francis Peck's death.'

On leaving the Dower House Pollard drove through Clearwell St Philip and on to the next village. Here he stopped at a telephone kiosk and put through a call to Scotland Yard. He asked for immediate enquiries to be made from the Paris police about the death of Geoffrey Parr in May or June 1960.

'The essential thing I want to get on to,' he explained, 'is who identified his body. My information is that he was yanked out of the Seine. I'll ring you back after lunch.'

Back on the road again he experienced a sense of anticlimax. Even if I can make Mrs Ridley admit that she was being black-mailed by Geoffrey Parr alias Geoffrey Palmer, he thought, will it turn out to be completely irrelevant to this bloody case?

Chapter 9

Toye had spent the period of Pollard's visit to Lady Boyd-Calthrop in systematically checking and rearranging the contents of the case file. He now sat listening to the account of the interview with head slightly inclined, an attentive owl in his large horn-rims.

'If it was Helen Parr who identified the body,' Pollard summed up, 'all things considered, it strikes me as just possible that it wasn't her husband's, and that George Palmer could have been Geoffrey Parr. If somebody else identified it, it probably was Parr's all right. Reverting to Palmer, his passport showed that he'd been in South Africa. If he was Parr, he may not even have known that Helen was dead, having walked out on her a couple of months before she died, according to Lady B-C. The fact that he went to the Wellchester Information Bureau and got a pamphlet about Fairlynch suggests that he'd heard something about its now being open to the public, and wanted to check up. Add to this his cross-examination of Alix, it seems to me conclusive that he'd been out of touch at any rate for a considerable time. Therefore he can't have had a local buddy who'd be prepared to muck up "Pictures for Pleasure" at the drop of a hat. On the other hand, a resurrected Geoffrey Parr would have had scope for blackmailing Mrs Ridley.'

'Are you going to tackle her about Palmer's identity?' Toye asked.

Pollard hesitated.

'If somebody other than Helen identified the body, no. If she did – well, I haven't decided yet that Palmer's identity isn't relevant to our case as far as I can see. I'll put it to the AC, of course, but I think he'll agree that there wouldn't be much point in stirring up ancient mud, now that both Helen Parr and Palmer are dead.'

Toye remarked that the late Detective Chief Superintendent Crowe, Pollard's first mentor in the CID, and something of a legend at the Yard, always used to say that you couldn't hope to get to the bottom of a difficult case until you'd cleared the ground.

'This is it,' Pollard said. 'I've never been able to get that dictum of the old boy's out of my system. All the same, we'll shelve

Palmer–Parr pro tem, and concentrate on our two remaining leads: unsupported statements from Tom Basing and Hugo Rossiter about their movements last Saturday night. Did you ring the landlord of the Spireford pub?'

Toye had. A snack would be laid on in the landlord's quarters if Superintendent Pollard cared to call in.

'How about Rossiter?' he asked.

'I wish I knew,' Pollard sat scowling heavily. 'We know motive's a dirty word in our shop, but unless the chap's round the bend and no one's even noticed it, what conceivable motive could he have for mucking up "Pictures for Pleasure"? As to opportunity, I suppose he could have got back to Spireford far enough ahead of Gilmore and the others to dump his car somewhere and arrive at the Manor at the same time or soon after, and slip in by making a row in the garden or something which would bring Peck out again after Gilmore had gone. But even then, there's the library key problem.'

'He'd been working there a lot hanging the pictures. Mrs Peck said her husband never let the key out of his possession, but there might have been the odd chance of taking an impression, don't you think?'

'The argument against that is that it suggests the job was carefully worked out in advance,' Pollard said, 'while it seems much more like something done almost on the spur of the moment. Hence the Peck tragedy. Look here, I suppose Gilmore wasn't involved too? Suppose he called out to Peck just as he was driving off, and got him to come across to the car, leaving the front door open? Rossiter could have slipped in then. It wouldn't have taken more than a minute, and Gilmore could still have passed the lodge and got home when he had witnesses to say he did... This is pure theorising without a vestige of data, isn't it? Old Man Crowe would have hit the roof. What we could do, after researching into Basing's activities on Saturday night, is to see how long it would have taken Rossiter to get up to the front door of the Manor after arriving home from the party. There's a door on to the road from the bottom of the Fairlynch garden: I remember noticing it. You go out that way to the water garden on the other side. We'd better push off to the pub now.'

They arrived at The Waggoner in Spireford at half-past one. The bar was crowded, and curious eyes followed their progress in the wake of the landlord, Bob Pedlar, to a door at the rear. He escorted them to a small room with a table laid for a meal, and promised to return shortly with a couple of pints of Waggoner Special.

'The Scotland Yard gentlemen for a bit of lunch, Elsie,' he shouted in the direction of the open kitchen door before disappearing.

Mrs Pedlar, a fair woman with rosy cheeks hurried in to say that she would have a dish of ham and eggs on the table in two twos if the gentlemen would take a seat. Pollard recognised something familiar in her face, but for the moment could not place her. Before he could consult Toye, Bob Pedlar was back with the Special, announcing that he'd be glad to tell them anything he could when he had cleared everyone out at two o'clock. All Spireford was up in arms about poor Mr Peck.

The ham and eggs were whisked on to the table, and they were instructed to give her a shout when they were ready for their afters.

'I should think it's about a hundred to one that Basing's a non-starter, but anyway we're getting some decent country grub,' Pollard remarked, helping himself liberally. 'I'm sure I've seen Mrs Pedlar before some-where. Does she ring a bell with you?'

Toye agreed that she had a look of somebody, but he could not place her either. They ate heartily, the ham and eggs being followed by rhubarb pie and cream and a pot of tea. A door slammed and sounds of revving up came from the car park. Finally Bob Pedlar's head came round the door.

'You gentlemen mind if I bring my plate in along o' you?' he asked.

'We'd be glad,' Pollard assured him. 'Bring yourself a pint of the Special with it. What about Mrs Pedlar?'

'She'll be along presently.'

'Well, bring something for her, then.'

As soon as Bob Pedlar was installed at the table, Pollard announced that he would come to the point.

'I don't want to take up more of your time off than I must,' he said. 'It's about last Saturday night, of course. You were pretty busy, I expect?'

Bob Pedlar agreed that there had been a good crowd in. There always was on a Saturday night.

'You've probably been asked all this before,' Pollard went on, 'but we Yard blokes do like to get information at first hand. Were there any strangers in?'

'Not what you could rightly call strangers, sir. What there was had been brought by

234

regulars. Their relatives and friends, see?'

'We're specially interested in the hour between ten and eleven. You have a Saturday night extension, I expect.'

'Closing time's ten-thirty Saturday nights. Matter of fact we didn't pack it in till half-past twelve last Saturday. Private party, o'course,' he added hastily. ''Twas the wife's brother's birthday.'

'That's right,' confirmed Mrs Pedlar, who had come in and joined them. 'I'm sister to Tom Basing, who's head gardener up at Fairlynch.'

Pollard instantly saw the family likeness, while reflecting that he had never extracted information that he wanted quite so pain-lessly.

'I'm sure it was a good party,' he said. 'The fact that it didn't break up until half-past twelve could be useful to us. Did the guests go home on foot or by car?'

He learnt that everyone present was from the village. Tom Basing, his wife Rosie, and her sister who was on a visit to them had only to go a few doors down the street. Tom's married daughter and her husband and two boys were from the council estate further on, but it was no distance to go and not worth getting out a car.

'The Wellchester police came round asking if anybody'd seen a car go through the village late that night,' Bob Pedlar added, 'but nobody had. Somebody heard one pass at about half-past three, but it turned out to be the vet, going back from Manor Farm. Farmer Hayes was having a bit of trouble with a calving cow.'

Pollard marvelled once again at the efficacy of village grapevines. It seemed advisable to keep the conversation going in order not to let it appear that the birthday party had provided all the information he wanted. This was no problem. Reference to the events at the Manor brought a stream of comments from both the Pedlars, in which local residents featured prominently. He learnt nothing new, however, beyond the fact that there was much interested speculation about Hugo Rossiter's fairly frequent absences from home.

'Gives out he's going on painting trips,' Bob Pedlar said with a broad grin. 'Going on the tiles into the bargain, that's my guess.'

Elsie Pedlar clicked her tongue, but in merely token disapproval. Apparently Hugo Rossiter's obvious failings as described by Lady Boyd-Calthrop did not prevent him from being *persona grata* at The Waggoner.

After a discreet interval Pollard decided that he could bring the interview to an end, and extricated Toye and himself with thanks for some useful, if unspecified information, and reiterated praise of Elsie Pedlar's cooking and Waggoner beer.

'Well, that's that,' he remarked as they stepped out into the village street. 'The end of the Basing road. You'd better go and look at the church with the critical eye of a sidesman, while I ring the Yard to see if anything's come through from Paris.'

He strode down the street to the telephone kiosk by the Post Office, aware of interested scrutiny from behind curtains. A small boy sucking a lolly took up a vantage point by the letter-box. Pollard saluted him gravely and entered the kiosk.

Ten minutes later he emerged and went in search of Toye, whom he found in the church studying the inscriptions on the tombs of members of the Ridley family. Toye jerked his head in the direction of the vestry from which sounds of vigorous sweeping were coming, and they went out into the afternoon sunshine.

'All very cut and dried,' Pollard told him as they walked back to the car. 'On June the eleventh 1960 the body of an unknown man was retrieved from the Seine. He'd been stripped of everything but his vest and pants and beaten up. Descriptions were posted, and on June the twentieth he was identified as her husband by Mrs Helen Parr, who stated that he had left her two months previously. Both were British subjects. Enquiries established that the deceased was wanted by the British police in connection with a fraudulent company prospectus.'

'If the dead chap wasn't Parr, you'd hardly think she could have got away with it,' Toye commented.

'There must have been enquiries over here, of course. My guess is that "Parr" was an alias, and that he had a faked passport, and the police drew a blank when they checked up on the application for it. It all suggests that he was an unimportant figure in shady circles here, and bit off more than he could chew in the Paris underworld... All theory, of course.'

Toye switched on the engine and looked round enquiringly.

'The Manor, to re-enact Rossiter's possible movements after leaving Weatherwise Farm last Saturday night. I can't think of anything else at the moment that seems even remotely useful, can you?'

They found the drive gates closed and a notice announcing that Fairlynch Gardens would reopen on the following Monday, 10th April 1978 at 2.00 pm.

'We'll leave the car here,' Pollard decided. 'Less ostentatious. Pull in behind that mini.'

'It's that chap's again,' Toye said, as he parked neatly. 'The fatty with ginger hair who was at the window.'

'As usual you're right where a car's concerned,' Pollard said, getting out and inspecting the mini. 'So what? Mrs Ridley's over at Clearwell St Philip, lunching with the Dowager. I hope Fatty isn't making a nuisance of himself to young Alix. We'll keep a look out for him.'

The lodge was apparently deserted, and they walked up the drive towards the Manor. The warm still air was heady with the scent of daffodils and narcissi, and the only sound was the cooing of wood pigeons overhead. Quite suddenly as they approached the house the front door burst open, and Kit Peck hurried purposefully in the direction of the steps leading down to the car park.

'What goes on?' Pollard said, at the same time quickening his pace. 'Let's follow discreetly.'

At the top of the steps they both stopped dead at the sight of the young man standing beside the ticket office and listening intently. The next moment Kit sensed their approach and beckoned urgently, at the same time making a gesture enjoining silence. Moving swiftly and soundlessly they reached him within a couple of seconds.

'You're talking absolute rot,' Alix Parr was saying indignantly. 'What's it got to do with my grandmother, anyway?'

In spite of her vehemence Pollard detected underlying anxiety.

'I'm not talking rot,' replied the flat nasal voice of the encounter outside the lodge, but with an unmistakeably gloating note. 'Anything but, so you'd better listen. You've seen it in the paper about that chap who pinched a car in Wellchester last Saturday night, drove it to Brynsworthy, pinched another, crashed it and killed himself? A criminal on the run all right, and the fuzz are trying to find out who he was. He had a tenner on him, and they've published its number. Now then, I'm a careful sort of bloke. When I pay out tenners I note down the numbers. You never know when it might come in useful: help towards promotion or whatever... I paid out that tenner myself, see? To your high and mighty grandmother.'

The voice ended on a triumphant note. There was a short tense silence.

'You're nuts,' Alix said briefly. 'Dozens of people must have had it between Gran and the man. And don't talk about her in that beastly rude way, you rotten little twit.'

'Easy,' the voice replied unpleasantly, 'seeing I hold the trumps. I paid it out at our Wellchester branch just as we were closing, a week ago yesterday. In she came and cashed a cheque, pretending not to know who I was. Then the manager came out and was all over her – Mrs Ridley this and Mrs Ridley that – and she told him she was on her way home, and wanted some cash as she'd been doing a lot of shopping and cleared herself out.'

'Anybody who isn't a complete nit would see that she must have filled up with petrol on the way home. What are you trying to prove? That she's in with criminals?' Alix demanded contemptuously.

'I don't need to *prove* anything. Just give the Press a story. They'll do the rest. Might even pay me.'

'Even you couldn't do such a – a filthy low-down thing as that.'

'Couldn't I? A worm'll turn, you know.

241

There's a way out, though, if you don't want grandma all over the cheap papers. Like to know what it is?'

As tension built up inside the ticket office the pungent smell of recently applied creosote made Pollard's nose tickle violently. He rubbed it hard with the back of his hand and buried it in his handkerchief. Toye glanced at him solicitously.

'You must be tight,' Alix was saying a little breathlessly, 'unless you're on pot or something. Push off! Nobody asked you to come here, and the gardens aren't open, anyway... Don't come any nearer, either. You make me feel sick.'

There was a distinctly unpleasant laugh.

'I'm not pushing off till you've made up your mind, Alix dear. You can choose. I'm going straight back from here to the *Evening News* office in Wellchester. The editor and I are buddies, and I'm offering him one of two scoops. Either one on your precious grandmother and her tenner, or one on our engagement. Headline stuff, both of 'em. It's up to you.'

Kit Peck with an unsuspected set to his jaw moved a step forward. Inside the ticket office there was the sound of a sudden scuffle and a scream from Alix.

'Get away! Don't touch me!'

Before the words had died away Kit was round at the door of the ticket house with a string of epithets that caused Pollard fleeting surprise. He arrived with Toye in time to see a figure in a grey suit crash landing in a nearby clump of rhododendrons.

'In the classic phrase,' he said, 'what's going on here? Inspector, get whoever's in those bushes on to his feet, will you?'

A dishevelled young man, scarlet in the face, was helped up. His spectacles were retrieved by Toye and handed to him. Trembling with shock and rage, he pointed to Kit Peck who was leaning against the wall with folded arms.

'That man assaulted me! You saw him – you're both witnesses. I'll take him to court. I'll...' Suddenly recognising Pollard and Toye he broke off.

'Mr Peck, do you admit this assault?' Pollard asked in the dead silence which followed.

'I do,' Kit Peck replied complacently. 'I socked the blighter one on the jaw, and chucked him into the bushes.'

'Unusual behaviour on Heritage of Britain property,' Pollard commented. 'If he takes you to court as he proposes, have you a plea of provocation?'

'He was trying to blackmail my fiancée.'

A quick gasp was audible from the interior of the ticket office.

'He was threatening to tell the editor of the *Wellchester Evening News* that Mrs Ridley had given a ten pound note to a car thief. A note that he'd paid out to her in the Bank where he works. He said he was going straight back to let them have either this scoop or the news of his engagement to Miss Parr.'

'It's an absolute lie,' blustered the victim of the assault. 'It's your word and hers against mine. You've no witnesses.'

'That's where you're mistaken,' Pollard informed him. 'There were two witnesses, both CID officers who listened in to the conversation. Inspector Toye and myself. Your name, please?'

The scarlet had ebbed from Charles Hindsmith's face leaving a greenish tinge, the result of physical shock and acute apprehension.

'I refuse to answer,' he muttered.

'He's called Charles Hindsmith.' Alix Parr had emerged from the ticket office, with, Pollard noted, a striking increase in poise and confidence. She was standing beside Kit Peck, whose arm was protectively round her shoulders. 'He works in the Southern Counties bank at Wellchester, and comes out to the Spireford branch on Thursdays.'

Pollard eyed him dispassionately.

'You're in a nasty spot, Mr Hindsmith,' he observed. 'The law takes a very serious view of blackmail.'

'It was only a joke,' Charles Hindsmith gabbled desperately. 'Of course I wasn't serious. I was only trying to – to show Alix I cared about her. I didn't know she was engaged to him.' He gave Kit Peck a malevolent look. 'Why's it been kept dark, anyway?'

'Hardly your business,' Pollard pointed out. 'Are you bringing an assault charge against Mr Peck or not?'

'Wouldn't I enjoy answering to it in court?' Kit Peck enquired of no one in particular.

'Yes or no, Mr Hindsmith? Don't waste our time.'

'No!' Charles Hindsmith shouted. 'He's a thug with no sense of humour, and not worth bothering about.'

'A wise decision under the circumstances,' Pollard told him. 'At the same time, I advise you to revise your own sense of humour if you want to keep out of real trouble.

Inspector, would you take Mr Hindsmith to his car, and get a full statement from him about this ten pound note for the Brynsworthy police? Then start on the job we had lined up for this afternoon. I'll join you later.'

'Certainly, sir... This way, please, Mr Hindsmith.'

As Toye escorted his unwilling companion in the direction of the drive, Pollard turned to find Kit and Alix wholly absorbed in each other.

'My congratulations,' he said, and was unable to resist the temptation of adding that he had had no idea that they were engaged.

They looked self-conscious, and Alix went attractively pink.

'Gran doesn't know yet,' she said hastily. 'We've only just decided.'

'Actually we shan't get married yet,' Kit added. 'Not until Alix is back from Canada. She might come across a bloke there she'd rather have.'

They exchanged another long glance.

'When are you going to tell Mrs Ridley?' Pollard asked patiently. 'I rather want to get a bit of information from her this afternoon. I'll be the soul of discretion about you two, of course. Is she at home?'

'She's been out to lunch,' Alix said, looking at her watch. 'She'll be back soon if she hasn't turned up already. Listen!'

A distant barking was audible.

'Terry. She took him with her, and they're back.'

'Suppose you two go for a walk in the woods, and give me time to call on her first?' Pollard suggested.

'That's what I call an idea,' Kit said.

'Me too,' Alix agreed. 'We'll break it to her that we're engaged this evening; and you can find out what she did with that ten pounds.'

'Yes, we'll get that straightened out,' Pollard assured her. 'I don't think you'll have any more trouble with Mr Hindsmith, on that or any other subject.'

Alix grinned.

'Sorry I went all maidenly and yelled when he tried to embrace me, but honestly, he's the end. You were super, Mr Pollard – sorry, bad joke!'

'Rotten,' Kit agreed. 'Thanks a million from both of us though,' he added with sincerity, wringing Pollard's hand.

They set off in the direction of the woods. Pollard watched them out of sight, and then turned and began to walk slowly across the car park towards the drive. He considered several possible openings to his interview with Katharine Ridley, but finally discarded them all, deciding to play it by ear.

The front door of the lodge was ajar, and his arrival was greeted by an outburst of barking which brought Katharine Ridley to the threshold. She looked informal and charming, he thought, in a spring suit with her hair beautifully set, and greeted him without a trace of apprehensiveness.

'Do come in,' she said. 'I'm just back from lunch with an old friend. I don't know where Alix has got to. Do you want to see her too?'

'No, not this time, thank you,' Pollard said, following her into the sitting room, and taking a chair facing her own at the open window. He looked at her, relaxed, assured and gay, and suddenly hated his job. At the same moment he decided to plunge straight in.

'Mrs Ridley,' he said gravely, 'the initials were right, weren't they, but not the name? Not George Palmer, I think, but Geoffrey Parr?'

She went so deathly white that for a moment he thought that she was going to faint.

'How did you find out?' she whispered at last.

'Partly through your telling me yourself by acting out of character over his visit. Your account of your movements last Saturday afternoon came unstuck, you see, when I checked it by questioning other people. Also, you were obviously in a state of tension when the visit was innocently mentioned by Alix, and miraculously restored to your normal self as soon as his death in a car crash appeared in the Press. I was puzzled about what the link between you and this George Palmer could be. Then, almost by chance, I learnt the tragic story of your daughter Helen and the fact that Alix was an orphan from birth, and began to speculate, having checked dates.'

'Oh, God, I thought we'd be safe once he was dead,' Katharine Ridley said miserably, twisting her hands together.

'I haven't come here to threaten you with digging up the past,' Pollard told her, 'only to clear up once and for all what has been a distracting false lead in the enquiry into Mr Peck's death. How long have you known that Geoffrey Parr was still alive?'

'How long?' She stared at him in blank astonishment. 'Why, only since last Saturday, although looking back, it's felt like years. When he suddenly came up to me in the gardens I thought I was going to die from the sheer horror of it.'

'Had he come to blackmail you?'

She nodded.

'He wanted money – five thousand pounds. He threatened to take Alix back to the woman he was living with if I didn't give it to him. I knew he couldn't because he was legally dead. But – but she'll be of age in August … it was her reaction to knowing he was her father that I was afraid of.'

'Yes, I see,' Pollard said thoughtfully. 'The serious-minded young's idealism makes them terribly vulnerable, doesn't it? Did you actually give Geoffrey Parr any money last Saturday?'

'I gave him thirty pounds. He was pretty well down and out. He said he's been in South Africa all this time, and had done quite well out there at first, but things had got difficult and some of his friends had taken risks over shady deals and were in trouble with the police. Obviously he'd been involved too, but managed to get out before he was arrested. He was that sort of man all along. That's why he suddenly married my poor Helen and rushed her over to Paris in the spring of 1960. It all came out when the French police made enquiries over the identification. But I suppose the English police hadn't a definite case against him, only suspicions, and as he was dead – or so they accepted – they didn't bother to check up any further. No relatives ever came forward, and the police in London thought Parr wasn't his real name.'

'Going back to the money you gave him,' Pollard said after a pause, 'it was in cash, I expect?'

'Yes. One ten pound and two five pound notes, and ten ones. Fortunately I had cashed a cheque for fifty pounds in Well-chester on Friday afternoon.'

'Do you remember the cashier who paid it out?'

Katharine Ridley looked puzzled.

'Yes, I do. It was a tiresome young man called Charles Hindsmith who's been pestering Alix. I gave him pretty short shrift once when he rang her up, and always avoid him at the Bank. But it was just on closing time and he was the only cashier free. I pretended not to notice him.'

'This afternoon,' Pollard said carefully, 'he was socked on the jaw and thrown into the rhododendrons by the ticket office by young

Mr Peck.'

Katharine Ridley gasped.

'He wasn't trying to rape Alix, was he?'

'Oh, no. Nothing as drastic as that. But he had been making a rather inept attempt to blackmail her into announcing her engagement to him. You see, he had made a note of the numbers of the ten pound notes he paid out to you, and one of them was found on Geoffrey Parr. Its number had been released to the Press and he recognised it. Of course he's got the wits to realise that he has no proof that you gave Parr the note: it could perfectly well have gone into circulation through your spending it, but he was in a position to make unpleasant publicity for you.'

Katharine Ridley's sharp intake of breath was audible.

'But surely he'll do it all the more after Kit Peck's onslaught? How did Kit come to be there?'

'He must have seen Hindsmith come to the ticket office and gone down to turn him out as the gardens are closed. Inspector Toye and I came on to the terrace just as Mr Peck went into action rather quickly, and Hindsmith was extricated from the rhododendrons to learn that his attempt at blackmail had been overheard by two officers of Scotland Yard. He's a very frightened young man, and you needn't anticipate any further trouble from him. My guess is that on Monday morning he'll put in an application for a transfer to another branch of his Bank.'

'What can I possibly say to Alix about all this?'

'That's a matter for your own judgement, Mrs Ridley,' Pollard told her. 'There's one question I'd very much like to ask you, if I may. Why did your daughter identify another body as her husband's?'

'At this distance of time,' Katharine said slowly, 'I can see in a way that it was all our fault. We didn't realise how the war had changed the world. She reacted violently against all my husband and I stood for, and I shall always think that she married Geoffrey Parr as a – a sort of supreme gesture of protest and defiance, if you understand me. Then he let her down and she wanted to blot him out in – well, despair. I'd like to show you her photograph.'

Pollard studied the studio portrait of a girl of about eighteen. It was a striking face, combining, he thought, the tenacity of the Young Heir and Alix with an exaggeration of

Katharine Ridley's vitality and impulsive-
ness: a highly explosive mixture.

'Thank you,' he said. 'By the way, Alix has
gone for a walk with Kit Peck. I forgot to tell
you.'

Their eyes met.

'He's so dull and worthy,' she said.

'If you had heard his language just now,
and seen his onslaught on the wretched
Hindsmith,' he told her with the vestige of a
grin, 'I think you might revise that opinion.'

Toye was sitting at the wheel of the Rover
writing up his notes.

'Palmer *was* Parr,' Pollard said, subsiding
into the passenger seat. 'I got the whole
story out of Mrs R without any difficulty.
This is what happened...'

Toye was severely critical of what he considered lack of thoroughness on the part of
both the French and the British police.

'Well, it's old history,' Pollard pointed out.
'I don't believe that the AC will want anything done about it after all this time. It's not
as if there are known Parr relatives – probably Parr was another alias. And no money's
involved. And as far as we're concerned the
whole affair's irrelevant... How did you get
on?'

Toye reported that he had begun by having a look at the door in the wall at the bottom of the Fairlynch main garden. It gave on to the road, just opposite the gate into the water garden on the far side. It had no lock but two bolts on the inside.

'There's a notice on the inside saying that the water garden won't be open until April the thirtieth,' Toye went on, 'so people wouldn't have been going through last Saturday afternoon. But Rossiter could easily have nipped down and slipped back the bolts after closing time. But even with this done, I don't reckon it could ever be proved that he had enough time to get up to the house and somehow slip in while Peck was talking to Gilmore when they got back from the party. Anyway, wouldn't this imply that Gilmore was on the job, too?'

'Never mind about that at the moment,' Pollard said. 'Let's concentrate on the timing to start with.'

Toye argued that this depended on two things. How much start did Rossiter have when he left Weatherwise Farm? Gilmore said 'about five minutes'. They had been putting food into the Gilmore car, and wouldn't have been looking at their watches. Then neither Mrs Ridley nor Alix was definite about how long it was before the car came back from the Manor after dropping Francis Peck. All they could say was that it came back very soon. Gilmore himself said that he had talked to Peck for a couple of minutes.

'Then there's the question of Rossiter's car,' Toye went on. 'He couldn't have left it in the road, which is narrow just there. Gilmore would have had to slow down, and the others would have noticed it. He didn't leave it inside the gate of his own place, because Mr Howlett stopped there and had a look at about eleven thirty on Saturday night, thinking he might have got to Manor Farm. He said there was a bit of a haystack and some machinery under a tarpaulin, but not a car. I thought I'd better check up properly, so I walked right down to the old mill where Rossiter lives. There didn't seem to be anyone in, so I belted all the way back, along the road, through the garden door and up all the steps to the top terrace. Hardly got my breath back yet. It took me eight minutes. All things taken into account, I wouldn't have thought he could have made it in the time if he'd driven right home first. And if he didn't, what did he do with his car?'

'I hope you remembered to go down and bolt that garden door again,' Pollard remarked after a pause.

Toye turned and stared at him. Then a grin spread over his normally serious face.

'Sorry old boy,' Pollard told him, 'but I couldn't resist it. No, you're dead right, of course. As evidence it's all hopelessly inconclusive. At the moment we haven't a single lead to work on – let's face it.'

They sat on in a heavy silence. Presently Toye observed that they had been badly stuck before.

'I'll tell you what else we've done before when bogged down,' Pollard said suddenly. 'Gone home. Let's head for town. Some things look better from a distance.'

Chapter 10

In the Pollard household the morning of Easter Sunday was strenuous. An exciting breakfast, with boiled eggs appropriately decorated for each member of the family by Jane, was followed by the hasty unwrapping of Easter eggs proper and a dash to church by car. On the return there was a lightning change into picnic clothes for the twins who were being taken down to the coast by neighbours. Soon after eleven their parents waved off a jubilant car load.

'Peace, perfect peace, bless their little hearts,' Pollard remarked as they went back into the house, 'the only snag being that we've both got urgent jobs on hand.'

'Infuriating, isn't it?' Jane agreed. 'Still, at least you're at home. And I suppose I might win a luxury weekend for two in Paris if I can only get this wretched poster done for the comp. It's got to be in by Thursday. There's masses of food laid on, by the way, so we can have separate lunch breaks if it fits better.'

Shortly afterwards Pollard watched her go down the garden to the studio he had improvised for her over the garage. He collected the file of the Fairlynch case without enthusiasm, and settled himself in an armchair by the open French window of the sitting room. A profound Sabbath calm seemed to have descended on the neighbourhood, even the roar of non-stop traffic on main roads not far distant being muted. It was pleasantly warm, and for a couple of minutes he gazed out into the garden watching a thrush engaged in a systematic worm hunt on the lawn. Then with an effort he brought his mind to bear on the intransigent problems confronting him, and started to clear the decks in the tradition of the late Chief Superintendent Crowe.

People with satisfactory alibis could be eliminated: Tom Basing, Farmer Hayes, the Cootes and the Allbrights. So could Katharine Ridley and Alix on the grounds of being psychologically and physically incapable of knocking out Francis Peck and transporting him to the boiler house. The same obviously applied to Lady Boyd-Calthrop, who, like the Allbrights and Cootes, was involved in 'Pictures for Pleasure', and had had her exhibit stolen. On considering the two Gilmores,

Pollard decided that they could only be provisionally eliminated at present. Malcolm Gilmore's return from the Manor within a few minutes of dropping Francis Peck there had not actually been seen by the inmates of the lodge, who had merely heard his car pass. His arrival home shortly afterwards depended entirely on his wife's evidence. In theory Malcolm could have helped Hugo Rossiter slip into the Manor unobserved by Francis Peck.

So what, Pollard thought gloomily? Two people whose alibis were not cast-iron, one possible suspect with doubtful opportunity and no apparent motive, and a person or persons unknown of whom there had not been the faintest hint or trace up to date.

The least unpromising course seemed to be to concentrate on Hugo Rossiter. Pollard leant back in his chair and shut his eyes, reliving the meeting with him at Fairlynch Manor and the conversation with the astute Lady Boyd-Calthrop... A physically powerful chap, he thought, visualising the tall strongly-built figure. Big features, tightly-curling black hair, eyes that didn't miss much. A powerful personality, too, full of the confidence born of real and recognised ability, a sense of humour running through the assertiveness. Lady Boyd-Calthrop had filled in the portrait with acumen: attractiveness to women, generosity to friends within the limits of a basic selfishness, impatient intolerance of frustration, but above all, intelligence. A coat-trailer where the Establishment was concerned, but a good mixer in The Waggoner. A chap who enjoyed taking chances...

Opening his eyes again, Pollard began to consider a potential case against Hugo Rossiter. He fulfilled the initial requirements of a knowledge of the Manor and its grounds, and he had been closely involved with 'Pictures for Pleasure' from the start. Toye's reconstruction had shown that he might have been able to arrive in the region of the Manor's front door at the time when Malcolm Gilmore and Francis Peck returned from the party at Weatherwise Farm. 'Might', however, was the operative word. As things stood at the moment it was not possible to prove that he could have made it. The fact that he was not a professional thief could tie up with the apparently amateurish character of the whole operation.

It was, of course, the question of motive that was so baffling where Rossiter was concerned. As far as an attempted theft of the Ridley portrait went there appeared to be none. It was not an outstandingly good work of art, it was virtually unsaleable, and there was not a shred of evidence of hostility towards Katharine Ridley – quite the reverse. The removal of five pictures from the exhibition merely to deposit them a short distance away seemed just as motiveless. If the idea had been to annoy their owners, why had the Ridley portrait been interfered with? Not as a blind, unless the five pictures had been the real object of the robbery all along, and the thief had counted on being able to return and pick them up shortly. But didn't this tell in Rossiter's favour, though? He lived almost on the doorstep of the Manor, and could easily have taken them home that night. It would have been a senseless risk to return to collect them later. And what the hell would he have wanted them for, anyway, Pollard asked himself savagely, mentally reviewing the quintet?

He gave an involuntary start at a sudden scrabbling up the back of his chair. The next moment Nox, the family's small black cat, arrived on his shoulder and then landed painfully on his knee.

'Keep your claws in, damn you,' Pollard adjured him, rubbing himself.

Nox instantly impersonated a starving stray, uttering a thin plaintive mew and staring with desperate hunted eyes.

Pollard groaned, got up, and carried him into the kitchen. Here he poured out a saucer of milk, and filled another with some of the contents of a packet labelled Purr Plus. Nox sank down before the milk and began to lap in slow ecstasy. Pollard made a silent exit, closed the kitchen door and returned to his problems.

His thoughts took up where they had left off, reverting to the stolen pictures. Of all the odd features of the case, their removal and subsequent dumping so near at hand with no real attempt at concealment were perhaps the most bizarre. Surely whoever had acted in this way would know that they would be held by the police when found? Could this have been the motive, to get them out of 'Pictures for Pleasure' for some reason? If...

Pollard's thought sequence suddenly snapped off short, broken by an inrush of inexplicable excitement. Then his mind began to race forward. If Rossiter had removed them, knowing that they would pass into police custody and not be hung for the time being, why had he included them in the first place? What could have made him change his mind about them when 'Pictures for Pleasure' had only been open for a single afternoon? Only some very urgent reason could have driven him to act as he did that night… Was there anything at all in Inspector Rendell's preliminary report that threw any light on this?

As he put out his hand to pick up the file, Pollard stopped dead, transported back in time to the first meeting with the Inspector and Superintendent Maynard. He sat very still in the shock of sudden illumination… 'A Professor Chilmark,' the Super had said, 'who advises HOB about pictures, was coming to have a private view on Sunday…'

Pollard released a pent-up breath. When was the time of Chilmark's visit known? Was it fixed just before 'Pictures for Pleasure' opened? Could this have been the reason for the hastily planned character of the theft? Was the removal of the five pictures to ensure that Chilmark, an art expert, should not see them? Could Rossiter have discovered that one of them was very valuable and intended to steal it, substituting a copy made by himself? Lady Boyd-Calthrop's 'Head of an Old Peasant' leapt to Pollard's mind, only to be dismissed. Professor Chilmark knew this picture, and had said that she would be lucky to get £500 for it. And he was a recognised expert: impossible that Rossiter should have been more knowledgeable...

Absently rubbing his forehead with the back of his hand, Pollard reviewed the other pictures. 'Inspiration' and 'Oleanders on Lake Lugano' could be written off at once. 'Frosty Morning' was in a different class, but surely Rex Allbright, whose knowledge of pictures had so impressed Toye, would have realised it if he possessed an early-twentieth-century masterpiece? That left the Gilmore's 'Flight into Egypt'.

Once again Pollard found that he was holding his breath. Suppose Malcolm Gilmore's great-uncle, anxious to cut a dash as a painter had got hold of a genuine Old Master and passed it off as his own work? Rossiter might have discovered this when vetting exhibits for 'Pictures for Pleasure', and decided to carry out a substitution and sell the original. His copy might not have been ready at the time of the opening, and the news of Professor Chilmark's visit on the following day would have meant either scrapping the substitution scheme for good and all, or somehow removing the painting for an appreciable time. It was easy to see

that to a man of Rossiter's ability and temp-
erament the second course would have a
strong appeal.

As usual after a flash of inspiration
Pollard's excitement began to ebb as flaws
presented themselves. He wondered if it
were credible that the Gilmore family could
have possessed a valuable Old Master for
over a century without discovering the fact.
On the whole he felt that it was a possibility.
The present generation clearly had some
interest in art, but did not strike him as
people with a genuinely knowledgeable
background. Then there was still the problem of whether Rossiter could have got into
the Manor on the Saturday night. If
Malcolm Gilmore had helped him in some
way, it would mean that they were both in
on the substitution plan...

After turning this idea over in his mind
Pollard decided that it had advantages over
his original one. After all, the two men were
quite close friends, and Rossiter was said to
be generous to his friends. That he would
have robbed and cheated Gilmore somehow
did not ring true. It might be that 'Flight
into Egypt' was really valuable in the grand
manner, and the scheme was to smuggle it
out of the country without applying for an

export licence, on the grounds that it was merely a family souvenir of no commercial value, to be passed over to relatives living abroad, in Canada or the USA, for instance. As the owner of a building construction firm there would be conferences which it would be perfectly reasonable for Malcolm Gilmore to attend...

Guiltily aware of theorising without established facts Pollard pulled himself up. The time had arrived to find out if there was any solid evidence for the substitution idea. 'Flight into Egypt' must be vetted by the art forgery experts at the Yard. Using scientific techniques they would discover if it was a seventeenth- or eighteenth-century painting or one merely dating from the late-nineteenth-century. It was equally important to discover who Lecci was, if he had painted a 'Flight into Egypt', and if so, what was known of its subsequent history.

To save time while they call in one of the art experts they've got lined up, I'll try Chilmark, Pollard thought with sudden decision, getting up to search in the telephone directory. He found that by a stroke of luck the Professor lived in Kensington, not on the south coast or the outer margin of the commuter belt. Of course he might very well be away for Easter, or anyway out to lunch... Realising that he himself was hungry, Pollard looked at his watch. It was a quarter past one, an obviously unsuitable moment for ringing. He decided to wait until two o'clock. If Chilmark was at home he should have finished eating by then, but not yet sunk into Sunday afternoon lethargy.

He headed for the kitchen, and had just settled down to a wedge of veal and ham pie and some salad when Jane appeared in her painting smock, hair ruffled and nose shiny, but with an unmistakeable air of satisfaction.

'It's going to tick,' she said, collecting food for herself, and refraining in accordance with her invariable rule from enquiring about his own progress.

Their eyes met.

'I get the message,' she said.

'Only a faint gleam,' Pollard told her. 'I want to get hold of Professor Chilmark. I thought I'd call him at two on the chance that he's at home. From the address it's a pricey flat in Kensington.'

Jane nodded, and they ate hungrily in companionable silence.

Punctually at two o'clock Pollard dialled Professor Chilmark's number, steeling himself to disappointment as he listened to the ringing tone. Then the slightly dry elderly voice that he remembered repeated the number.

'Professor Chilmark? This is Chief Superintendent Pollard speaking. I must begin by apologising for calling you at this really outrageous moment.'

'No need to apologise, Superintendent. The call suggests a potentially exciting development. Is it in order to ask if it's connected with the matter we were discussing when we last met?'

'It is,' Pollard replied. 'I think you may be able to give me some valuable help. Could I possibly come over and see you today?'

'Come and welcome. Join me for a cup of tea at four. In the meantime I shall indulge in fascinating speculations. About parking, now...'

On putting down the receiver Pollard felt at a loose end. There was a good hour to fill in before he need start. His brain recoiled from the prospect of milling over the case against Hugo Rossiter yet again, and the indisputable fact that the grass needed cutting was a handy escape route.

With an electric mower the job was undemanding and satisfying, and a neat striped pattern emerged as proof of his labours. Reluctantly Pollard decided that there was not enough time to do the edges as well. After changing into more conventional clothes he put his head round the studio door. Jane, deeply engrossed, gave him the V-sign and blew him a kiss. He descended to the garage, emerged cautiously into the mews and drove off towards London. Traffic was relatively light, and feeling mentally refreshed by his short break, he spent the journey in grouping the essential facts to be put before Professor Chilmark.

He had surmised correctly that the flat would be pricey. His host led him into a surprisingly large room which he referred to as the library. It had south and west windows with wide views. The walls were lined with bookshelves from ceiling to floor with the exception of a single space occupied by an oil painting of such quality that Pollard involuntarily stopped to look at it. A rutted country lane ran between tangled hedges, bathed in the evening sunshine of high summer. Tiny fleecy clouds floated in a luminous sky almost imperceptibly tinged with pink. In the hedges an occasional wild rose caught and emphasised their colour. With consummate skill the artist had combined a limpid freshness with the mellowness of a day moving to its close.

'Like it?' Professor Chilmark asked.

'It's miraculous!' Pollard ejaculated. 'Whose is it?'

'I picked it up in France in '45 as an *"après Manet"*.'

Pollard opened his eyes wide.

Tea was set out in one of the windows.

'My housekeeper's off on Sundays,' Professor Chilmark said, switching on an electric kettle, 'but since my wife died I've become quite reasonably domesticated. Come and have a cup while we talk.'

A few minutes later they faced each other across the tea table. Told to help himself, Pollard took a sandwich.

'This is most awfully good of you,' he said.

'The debt's on my side,' Professor Chilmark replied. 'As I told you I'm a detective novel addict, and I've felt all along that Fairlynch was likely to beat most of 'em hollow. It's not the missing heir after all, is it?'

'There's been a missing liability who confused the issue to start with, but he turned out an irrelevance... I'm not sure how clued up you are on the developments since we first met?'

'I'm pretty sure I haven't missed anything that's appeared in the reputable Press, but bring me up to date, there's a good chap.'

Pollard put down his cup and sat back.

'On the morning after we met at your friends' house,' he began, 'a completely unexpected thing happened. The five paintings missing from "Pictures for Pleasure" were found by one of the Fairlynch under-gardeners in an unlocked shed at the top of the woods behind the house...'

He talked on, surprised at the ease with which a coherent account of the enquiry's progress emerged. At intervals he glanced at the intelligent appraising face on the opposite side of the table. When he began to outline his newly-developed substitution theory as the motive for the robbery, he watched Professor Chilmark's intent expression become one of rapt enjoyment.

'Of course,' he said, finally, 'the backroom boys at the Yard can establish whether "Flight in Egypt" is one or several centuries old. What I've come to consult you about, Professor, is whether there was a painter called Lecci, and if so, whether there's any record of this particular picture by him.'

He got a long look, one element of which he recognised as admiration.

'Certainly there was an early-eighteenth-century painter called Lecci,' Professor Chilmark replied emphatically. 'A Venetian. Respectable, but not of the first water. Hold on a minute, and I'll look him up.'

He got to his feet and walked over to one of the bookcases, extracted a large volume and carried it over to his desk. Pollard swung round and watched breathlessly as he consulted the index and turned pages.

'Here's the chap,' he said at last. 'Giacomo Lecci, 1680–1731 ... classical and religious themes in rococo landscapes ... fanciful architecture ... ruins ... relatively few works have survived ... h'm h'm ... small painting of the Flight into Egypt in cathedral of Portrova, North Italy...'

'What!' Pollard shouted. He found himself on his feet.

'Portrova,' Professor Chilmark repeated, surveying him with interest. 'Presumably you know it? Not one of North Italy's most attractive towns, in my view.'

Pollard was apologetic.

'Just for the moment a quite staggering coincidence seemed to have materialised,' he added.

'If I remember rightly, the cathedral at Portrova is dedicated to St Thomas,' Professor Chilmark remarked drily. 'Hold on a minute while I collect some drinks, and then let me hear about this coincidence.'

He left the room. Pollard stood at a window looking out unseeingly over a sea of roofs enclosing occasional green islands. He considered his course of action in the event of the Wellchester 'Flight into Egypt' really being an early-eighteenth-century painting. The chink of glasses roused him as Professor Chilmark reappeared, propelling drinks on a trolley.

'I can recommend this brand,' he said, holding up a bottle of whisky. 'Or would you prefer gin?'

Some minutes later Pollard put down a half-emptied glass appreciatively.

'If you can take another of my monologues, Professor,' he said, 'I'll be as brief as possible. My wife and I live in Wimbledon, not far from some close friends, a couple called Strode. David Strode is an up and coming solicitor. Last June they flew their car out to Milan, and set off on a fortnight's holiday in North Italy...'

As he described Julian Strode's experience in the cathedral in Portrova his misgivings mounted.

'Is it possible,' he asked on coming to the

end of the story, 'that if a copy was substituted for the genuine Lecci nearly a year ago nobody would have spotted it?'

Professor Chilmark was silent for some moments.

'Yes,' he said at last, 'I think it's quite possible. I had a look at the cathedral three years ago, and found it disappointing. It was very dark, and had a rather dusty derelict appearance, as if it had been left high and dry by the decline of traditional religious observance. Lecci is not a well-known painter, and only a comparatively few people would take the trouble to hunt down one of his pictures in the artistic *embarras de richesse* in that part of the world.' He broke off and looked at Pollard. 'I've no right at all to ask you this question, but what steps are you proposing to take in view of this link-up with Portrova?'

'It seems to me,' Pollard replied, 'that the significance – if any – of the Portrova link-up will be settled by the lab verdict on the Wellchester picture. I shall drive down to fetch it tomorrow and get it to the fake experts by the early afternoon. If it turns out to be the real thing, my next step will be to see my AC. I suppose in this case it might be difficult and pretty time-consuming to get the co-operation of the Italian authorities?'

'It certainly could be. But as it happens, the Regional Director in charge of the monuments and art treasures generally in the area is a personal friend of mine.'

The two men looked at each other. Pollard grinned.

'If you're free after lunch tomorrow by any chance,' he said, 'would you care to come along to the Yard?'

Twenty hours later, in the scheduled clinical atmosphere of a forensic laboratory at New Scotland Yard, Pollard found himself marginal to a small group of absorbed technicians closely watched by Professor Chilmark. 'Flight into Egypt', duly collected from Wellchester police station that morning, was being subjected to systematic testing to establish its approximate age and history. It was photographed with elaborate cameras, some incorporating microscopes. It was X-rayed. After lengthy discussion a minute quantity of solvent was applied to its bottom left-hand corner.

At this point Professor Chilmark detached himself from the group and came over to Pollard, rubbing his hands in satisfaction.

'Not a doubt in the world,' he told him.

'It's genuine early-eighteenth-century apart from the faked label on the back with old Gilmore's particulars. They're doing the full run of tests for the record, though. It'll be about another hour, I should think.'

Pollard nodded.

'Thanks,' he said. 'Here we go, then. I'll go on to the AC.'

He returned to the laboratory after a time and reported that the Assistant Commissioner would expect them at five o'clock.

'By the way,' he added, 'the AC's another of you people who are hooked on detective novels...'

The meeting, as Pollard told Jane later, went like a bomb from the word go. Professor Chilmark's presence had saved him from the usual comments about fancy cases with cloak and dagger touches. He had managed to get his substitution theory and the Portrova link across with just the right degree of conciseness.

'Good story, don't you think, sir?' Professor Chilmark had asked helpfully. 'Better plot than a good many on my own shelves.'

A literary diversion had followed, enjoyed by both participants, and the AC had surfaced from it reluctantly.

'Well, I suppose we'd better get down to

the matter in hand,' he said. 'I understand from Superintendent Pollard, Professor, that you've offered to go out to Portrova and pull a few wires. We'll pay all your expenses, of course. It's obviously essential to find out what's hanging in the cathedral as a genuine Lecci.'

After a short discussion it was arranged that Professor Chilmark should fly out to Milan on the following Wednesday. The AC turned to Pollard.

'You say you want to return to Wellchester and deal with various loose ends,' he asked.

'Yes, sir. If it turns out that the painting at Portrova is the copy of Lecci's original by Malcolm Gilmore's great-uncle, or a more modern fake, there seem to me to be three matters that we'd have to clear up before making a charge.'

'On presumably – assuming that a substitution of pictures has taken place – is why the hell Gilmore allowed the original to go to this "Pictures for Pleasure" show.'

'Exactly, sir. A second one is finding out if Gilmore or Rossiter or both were abroad in early June last year. The third is to discover how Rossiter got into both Fairlynch Manor itself and the library on the night of Francis Peck's death. It seems fairly obvious that

Gilmore distracted Peck's attention some-how, but at the moment there's no proof of how he managed it.'

'Well, I suppose you'd better go down and get these points cleared up, then,' the AC commented unenthusiastically. 'The sooner the better, that's all. Then the case can go into cold storage until Professor Chilmark gets back. I imagine you'll be in Italy for at least a week, Professor? It's extremely good of you to take this on for us.'

In reply Professor Chilmark was cau-tiously optimistic about the duration and outcome of his mission, and promised to keep in close touch.

Chapter 11

'You wouldn't have thought it was worth it,' Jane Pollard said suddenly in the middle of supper on Tuesday evening. 'For Rossiter and Gilmore, I mean. All the planning and the risk and the worry. It's not as though the Lecci is all that valuable. Wouldn't it have been pinched from Portrova cathedral by now if it was?'

'Probably,' Pollard replied, absently fiddling with a spare fork. 'You're right about the cash aspect. Chilmark thinks that twenty thousand would be the absolute maximum they could hope to net in the States. Ten thousand apiece tax-free's nice and handy, but not exactly a fortune these days. Personally, having met the two blokes and picked up quite a bit about them, I don't believe they were in it simply for the money.'

'So what, then?' Jane asked.

Pollard was silent for a moment and then looked up at her with a grin.

'The substitution idea was pure inspiration, you know. Brilliant, challenging and risky. Right up a chap like Rossiter's street. Enormous fun to pull off, nobody much the worse, and the Lecci much better looked after in some rich and not too scrupulous art lover's private collection. No violence or unpleasantness involved. Julian turning up at the critical moment and the Peck disaster couldn't possibly have been foreseen.'

'How do you suppose Rossiter got on to the original Lecci? Was he looking for it?'

'I think the odds are that it was pure chance. He goes on painting trips to Italy, and could have landed up in Portrova. It would have been the natural thing for an artist to take a look round the galleries and churches. Artists have good visual memories, and if he spotted the Lecci he'd have been struck by the resemblance to the Gilmore version. He'd consult a reputable guide book, vet the painting unobtrusively and come to the conclusion that it was the original copied by Great-uncle Gilmore. He's a quick thinker and wouldn't have taken long to see the possibilities of a swap, especially after observing the rather casual cathedral routine.'

'What about Gilmore? Has he got the same sort of mental make-up?'

'He hasn't anything like Rossiter's imagination and reckless streak, but he's a very competent bloke. I should expect the meticulous organisation behind the actual theft to be largely his contribution. He's got a bit of a one-track mind, too, and single-mindedness is a help to anybody planning a criminal enterprise. There's an outsize chip on his shoulder about official interference with profit-making in private enterprise. Scooping a cool ten thou tax-free would appeal to him immensely, as well as dodging the art export licence people.'

They sat in silence for a few moments.

'But would it be possible to prove that Rossiter and Gilmore were in the Portrova area at the time Julian was set on? It's nearly a year ago now,' Jane queried.

'With reasonable luck, yes,' Pollard replied. 'If Chilmark is satisfied that the painting now in the cathedral isn't the original Lecci, he's going to get the authorities on to hotel registration records. Proprietors are careful about passports and so on. But even if we can establish that the two chaps were within a reasonable distance of Portrova at the time, we're far from home and dry, as the AC won't hesitate to point out.'

There was another silence.

'I still think Rossiter and Gilmore were absolutely mad to do it,' Jane said emphatically. 'Especially Gilmore: he's got so much more to lose. You can go on painting when you come out of jail, but certainly not running a firm, even if you'd built it up yourself.'

Pollard agreed, yawning and stretching.

'Roll on, news from Portrova,' he said. 'It all depends on old Chilmark's findings.'

On the road to Wellchester the next morning, Toye expressed reservations about Professor Chilmark's trip to Portrova. He commented on amateurs who fancied themselves bringing home the bacon, and asked leading questions about the next move.

'We'll start,' Pollard replied, secretly amused, 'by making Maynard and Rendell do a spot of can-carrying. They can find out if Rossiter and Gilmore were away in early June last year. It's the sort of thing it's much easier for the local chaps to bring conversations round to. If you and I start ferreting about, people will start talking, and ten to one it'll get back to Rossiter and Gilmore. It doesn't do to underestimate those two, you know.'

'Escape routes lined up?' Toye asked.

'Yes, and plenty of ready cash at the end of the road... As to what we do next, I honestly don't know at the moment, old chap. Wait Micawberishly for something to turn up, perhaps.'

'In and out you get a real stroke of luck,' the habitually cautious Toye remarked unexpectedly, sweeping ahead of a Jaguar into the fast lane of the M4. 'Something you've never thought of in the way of a lead.'

Touched by this blatant attempt at encouragement, Pollard responded by reminiscing on bonanzas of this sort in some of their former cases.

At Wellchester Superintendent Maynard and Inspector Rendell reacted predictably. At first they were openly incredulous that two well-known local figures of the standing of Hugo Rossiter and Malcolm Gilmore could possibly be implicated in a serious crime. As Pollard put the facts before them, however, they unwillingly came round to admitting that a case against the pair was taking shape, and undertook to have enquiries made about their whereabouts in June 1977.

'I don't say we can do it at the drop of a hat,' Superintendent Maynard told them. 'Gilmore won't be much of a problem with all his employees, but Rossiter's more of a loner, and often off painting. Still, we'll do what we can.'

As he came out of the police station with Toye, Pollard made a sudden decision.

'Let's go out to Fairlynch and poke about,' he said. 'If Rossiter did the job, he left his car somewhere near the Manor, and we've got to find out where. It's as simple as that.'

On arriving they realised that a normal open afternoon was in full swing, with a surprising number of cars in the car park. Toye remarked that any sort of publicity paid off from the look of it. They returned to the drive and walked up to the house. As they arrived on the upper terrace the front door opened and a man of about forty came out, carrying some papers. He paused on seeing them, and Pollard raised his hat.

'Good afternoon,' he said. 'Are you the acting Warden, by any chance?', and introduced Toye and himself.

'David Harrow,' the man replied. 'I've been sent down from HQ to hold the fort until a new Warden's appointed.' He had a pleasant sensible face, and hesitated briefly. 'As a matter of fact I'm glad I've run into you. I've been debating trying to contact you. Could you spare a few minutes?'

'Certainly,' Pollard replied, inexplicably conscious of a faint tingle of excitement in the region of his spine. 'If you can help us in any way we'll be grateful.'

As they followed David Harrow into the house and up the staircase to the Warden's office he raised an eyebrow at Toye.

Facing them across a desk, David Harrow showed signs of diffidence.

'I'm probably wasting your time,' he said. 'I expect you get a lot of that from the public. But anyway, something that seems decidedly odd to me has happened, so here goes.'

As he spoke he stooped, opened a drawer in the desk, and extracted a large manila envelope. It contained a yellow folder of papers. The folder was stained with what looked like mud, and was stamped with the words GILMORE CONSTRUCTIONS LIMITED.

Pollard realised that he was holding his breath.

'I must explain,' David Harrow went on, 'that Heritage is considering converting part of the stable block into a tea room, and these people' – he tapped the folder – 'who are doing the alternations and so on here were asked for plans and an estimate. I'm due to take them up to the Finance Committee on Friday, so this morning I thought I'd better have a look at them and found them in this mess. I asked Mrs Peck if there was a duplicate set and she was simply baffled by the whole thing. It seems they arrived by post on the morning of Friday, April the first, and she and her husband went through them in detail that evening. She would have been in charge of the tea room, so naturally she was interested. It so happened that she came in here when her husband was putting them away and he made some remark about not having to think about them again until the meeting. I didn't want to bother her, so I said Mr Peck must have had them out to show somebody on the Saturday afternoon, and gone over to stables and accidentally dropped the folder in the yard. I also said I'd ring Gilmore Constructions and ask for another set.'

'And have you?' Pollard asked.

'Well no, actually. Not yet. Somehow I felt that there was something off-beat about it. You see, the tea room idea isn't public property, and Mr Peck was a most correct and discreet chap. And it isn't as though the situation here has been normal. So I thought I'd pass the buck, just on chance,' David Harrow ended rather lamely.

'I think it's possible that your instinct's been sound,' Pollard said, 'and we're glad to know about this matter. I'd like you now to do two things. First of all, hand over the folder to us for the moment. Inspector Toye will make out a receipt for it. Secondly, ring up Gilmore Constructions and ask for a duplicate. You're in a good position to say that you've hardly had time to get on top of things here yet, and the original set seems to have been mislaid. Perfectly convincing, and they are bound to have duplicates. And one more thing: I'd rather that this affair didn't leak out. You'll understand that I can't be more explicit at the moment.'

David Harrow grinned.

'It's desperately tantalising, but I take your point, of course.'

On leaving the Manor shortly afterwards, they returned to the car.

'So what?' Pollard said, when they were ensconced. 'For the first time we've got a possible link between Gilmore and Rossiter's getting into the Manor. It would have been perfectly normal – after Alix had been dropped at the lodge – for Gilmore to have asked Peck if he could have a quick look at the estimate about some point, or other. Peck would say that he'd go up to his office and get the folder if Gilmore would come in for a moment. Let's assume that Rossiter has managed to beat them to it, and is hiding round the side of the house. When Peck has gone upstairs, Gilmore opens the front door and lets him in.'

'Where'd he go?' Toye demanded. 'There's no cover in the hall?'

'If I'd been Gilmore,' Pollard said slowly, 'I'd have asked Peck to let me have the key to the library for a moment to see if Lydia had left her pen there when she wrote a cheque for that appalling picture in the afternoon. As soon as Rossiter was safely inside I'd come out again, with a pen I'd brought in my pocket, slam the door, lock it noisily, unlock it quietly and meet Peck in the hall, saying I'd locked up again. How's that? Don't tell me there's no supporting evidence at the moment. I know that. But is it logically sound?'

Toye was silent, carefully appraising the ideas put forward.

'I'd say it's logically sound,' he said at last, 'but not psychologically.'

'What on earth do you mean?'

'Well, we keep on hearing about Peck being so careful about security. Seems to me he'd have tried the library door to make sure that Gilmore had locked up properly.'

Pollard looked at his serious face with amusement.

'Haven't you ever felt a bit blurred after a good evening out, old man? The Gilmores do themselves pretty well from all accounts, and even young Alix admitted coyly to having had a few drinks. And don't forget that Peck had had the whale of a day.'

Toye reluctantly admitted that there could be a point there.

'Suppose he *had* tried the door and found it wasn't locked? There was the risk of Rossiter being locked in.'

'Pity it didn't work out that way. Peck would be alive now. Rossiter could have monkeyed about with the Ridley portrait, and then sloped off out of one of the windows with the five pictures. No risk, really... Look here, there aren't many people here now. Nip up and get a sample of any mud and earth you can find near the front door, and we'll get that folder tested at Wellchester.'

Toye collected a couple of sterilised containers and a palette knife from a case.

'I wonder how he came to drop the thing,' he said.

'He'd have come out to see Gilmore off in his car, probably still holding the folder and his keys. It was a windy night, remember. That keeps cropping up, doesn't it? I think it's quite possible that Peck had to make a grab at the front door when he opened it to go in again, and dropped the folder then. Gilmore would have driven away knowing nothing about it.'

Toye went off, and Pollard sat on in the Rover, his thoughts on Hugo Rossiter's return from the party at Weatherwise Farm. Quite suddenly he found himself acutely conscious of his own immediate surroundings, and contemplated the car park in some surprise. Then he remembered Toye's suggestion that the chap they were after might have parked there, well out of sight of the Pecks' windows, and used the car for his get-away during the night, coasting down the drive and out on to the road in neutral. The idea had been discarded on the strength of Tom Basing's statement that the car park was empty when he cut through it on his way home, after paying in his takings for the sale of plants during the afternoon. But suppose Hugo Rossiter had driven straight to it on leaving the Gilmores, and cut up the steps leading from the ticket office to the upper terrace? That would have been the easiest way of getting there before the Gilmore car arrived. But wouldn't Mrs Ridley have heard Rossiter's car go past the lodge? It was a difficult turn into the drive for anyone coming from the Weatherwise Farm direction, and one which would almost certainly have involved changing down...

At this point Toye reappeared.

'Get in,' Pollard said urgently. 'I've been hit by an idea – mainly yours rehashed.'

Toye listened carefully while it was expounded.

'I'd like to try coming in and going out to see how much row you'd have to make,' he said.

'O.K.,' Pollard agreed. 'While you're doing some trial runs I'll ask her if she heard a car come in shortly before Alix was dropped, and once again about cars in the night, although she told Rendell she hadn't heard any. And while I'm there, I'll see if I can find out if there was any difficulty in getting Gilmore to exhibit "Flight into Egypt".'

He went on ahead and found Katharine Ridley busy in her garden.

'I'm sorry to keep turning up, Mrs Ridley,' he said, smiling at her. 'There are just two bits of information I think you might be able to give me.'

'Don't apologise,' she said, driving a fork into the ground and coming towards him. 'I only hope I can tell you whatever it is. Shall we sit on this seat, or would you rather go indoors?'

'The seat would be fine,' he said. 'I get far too much indoors in London.'

When they were settled he came straight to the point, sensing that she was completely at her ease with him.

'I don't want to revive unhappy memories,' he told her, 'but could you just think back to the Saturday night when Alix was at the party and you were alone here? You were in bed, weren't you, and probably drowsy? Can you remember hearing another car go past shortly before Mr Gilmore's arrived bringing Alix home?'

Katharine Ridley shook her head decisively.

'If there was one,' she said, 'I didn't hear it consciously. After she had gone I was awake for some time, trying to decide what to do. Before I came to any conclusion I must have dropped off, because the slamming of a car door woke me, and I could hear her and Malcolm Gilmore and Francis Peck saying goodnight. I looked at my bedside clock which has a luminous dial, and it was just on half past ten... What *is* that car doing at this moment just out on the road?'

'I'm afraid that's Inspector Toye carrying out a small experiment. He won't be long.

Would you have heard a car starting up like that later in the night, do you think? It was a noisy windy night, apparently.'

'I only know I didn't hear one. Whether that means there wasn't one, or that there was and I slept through it, I just can't say.'

'Fair enough,' Pollard agreed. 'Now one more thing. It's about how you and Mr Rossiter got together the exhibits for "Pictures for Pleasure". I expect you drew up a plan of campaign, and either advertised or circularised likely lenders?'

'We were a bit more informal than that,' Katharine Ridley said. 'Actually the balloon went up at another of the Gilmores' parties, before I'd even had time to tell Hugo Rossiter that the HOB local committee wanted us to put on the show. People started ragging the Gilmores about their pictures and saying which we ought to have, and Lady Boyd-Calthrop stumped round in her inimitable way, laying down the law. I remember she said that we must have the "Flight into Egypt" for one, as religious pictures lent tone to an exhibition. Malcolm protested and said it was a ghastly daub by his great-uncle, but I backed her up for a quiet life, and so we had it. Thank heaven it has turned up again. After this Hugo and I drew up a list of people we thought would have reasonable pictures, and other people got to hear about it and offered to lend things. Some were quite frightful, of course, and we had to be tactful.'

'Thank you,' Pollard said. 'That's all very clear. Now I'll be off, and leave you to garden in peace.'

'One minute before you go,' Katharine Ridley said. 'I do want to thank you for all your understanding and kindness. And for helping me to come to terms with the Kit Peck–Alix situation, which I'm quite sure hasn't escaped your notice. Over the past two years I've been plotting and scheming frantically to stop it. Then somehow – I can't explain how – Geoffrey Parr's turning up made me see that I was making the same mistake that we did over Helen. Not realising how much the world had changed in Alix's lifetime, I mean. And then Kit came to see me, and I really felt rather ashamed. He's so good and wise for his age, and won't hear of a formal engagement until she's had her year in Canada.'

'It's good of you to tell me this,' Pollard said. 'I appreciate it very much. It's moments like this which make being a policeman bearable.'

He got up and held out his hand to her. As he went out to join Toye he thought regretfully of the distress which the solution of his case was bound to cause her.

Toye was waiting in the Rover.

'No go,' he said. 'Even in this bus you have to change down to get into the drive, and there isn't enough slope to keep you moving more than a few yards along the road when you coast out in neutral.'

'It all made more row than I'd have expected,' Pollard replied. 'And anyway, I'm satisfied that Mrs R didn't hear a car at either of the times we're interested in. But I managed to get on to something which throws a bit of light on why Gilmore and Rossiter ever let the genuine painting go to "Pictures for Pleasure". They seem to have been caught on the hop. According to Mrs Ridley the first they heard of the show was at a party at the Gilmores. That dominating old bird Lady Boyd-Calthrop was there, and proceeded to decide which of their pictures should be sent in. It seems that she specially picked on the "Flight". I don't think this is likely to have bothered Gilmore and Rossiter much because they simply must have had another convincing copy – done by Rossiter, presumably – to replace the genuine one when they eventually found a market for it.'

'Do you think Mrs Gilmore was in on the racket?' Toye asked.

'No, I don't. I may be wrong, but she strikes me as a woman with too much horse sense, apart from any other considerations. Gilmore must have said he was having his great-uncle's effort cleaned or something when he took it off to Portrova last year.'

'You'd think with all their careful planning they'd have had the substitute copy ready for "Pictures for Pleasure". Fancy falling down on that,' Toye commented critically.

'Pure guesswork on my part, but I think their scheme came unstuck over the frame. The great-uncle could have had an exact copy of Lecci's made by an Italian craftsman. Rossiter would have had to scrounge around junk shops and pick something up that he could adapt. I've noticed that early-eighteenth-century frames are standardised up to a point. They're gilded wood as a rule, with repeating patterns: flowers and shells and whatever. And Rossiter's art shop in Wellchester does framing. But it was a dicey job and finding a suitable old frame could very well have held them up. Rossiter had to put in a lot of time on the hanging, too... I say, let's go back to Wellchester and have a meal, and then do some thinking. It's no good just wandering round looking for places where Rossiter could have put his car that night...'

Later, after a satisfying supper, they wrote up their notes and then decided to call it a day. Toye hurried off to the last showing of a Western at a local cinema, a genre of film for which he had a surprising addiction. Pollard set off on an exploratory stroll in the historic centre of the city. After circling the cathedral and studying the statuary on its west front, he left the Close and spent some time on the medieval bridge over the river, now happily closed to motor traffic. He had found in the past that inspiration sometime dawned when his mind was tranquillised by watching drifting clouds or flowing water, but on this occasion none came. Finally he went back to the hotel, had a drink in the bar and decided on bed, still without a programme for the following day.

He woke to broad daylight, astonished that he had slept solidly through the night and had surfaced to find himself thinking of a witness whom he personally had not seen: the vet Howlett, interviewed by Toye. Lying in bed he wondered why? The chap had been quite definite about not having seen a car on or off the road during his journeys to and from Manor Farm. It might be worth interviewing him again, though. Sometimes a casual question produced a really valuable answer. At this point Pollard's mind began to visualise the entrance to the track leading to Mill Cottage. The track was rough and partly grass-grown. An electric fence kept in the young Friesian bullocks grazing in the field on the right. The field had hedges on the road and extreme right but was open to the Spire on the river side, beyond Mill Cottage's walled garden. Useful for watering the stock, Pollard thought, remembering his country childhood. The fag end of a haystack was on the left just inside the gate, with a tarpaulin casually thrown over it. The overall picture was clear enough, but somehow he felt vaguely dissatisfied. He looked at his watch and decided to get up.

Over breakfast Toye agreed that it might be worth seeing Howlett again, and went to the telephone to enquire about his surgery hours. They learnt that he would be on duty between nine and ten o'clock. Pollard looked in at the police station where a quietly triumphant Inspector Rendell informed him that they had already got Gilmore sewn up. It had turned out that a Sergeant Bland was engaged to Gilmore's secretary. He had taken her out on the previous evening and brought the conversation round to holidays. She had expressed hopes that her boss would take ten days off over the Bank Holiday at the end of May as he had last year, saying it had been a real rest cure for her.

'According to Bland he's a right bastard to work for,' Inspector Rendell added, 'and been worse than usual just lately.'

Pollard congratulated him on the quick result of his enquiries, and joined Toye in the Rover.

They found the waiting room of Mr Howlett's surgery crowded with animals and their escorts, but were told by the receptionist that they would be seen when the patient in the consulting room had been dealt with. A wave of hostility from the escorts greeted this statement.

'Where is your sick animal?' an indignant woman demanded in a deep voice.

Pollard replied with perfect truth that it had not been possible to bring him.

'All the animals here are under physical and mental stress,' the woman boomed. 'They should have priority.'

A loud cork-extracting pop came from a parrot's cage swathed in polythene. To

Pollard's immense relief the door of the consulting room opened, and a man emerged with a Pyrenean mountain dog on a lead. Under cover of a hostile demonstration from some of the other patients Pollard and Toye were ushered in.

Pollard like Mr Howlett on sight. He was young with untidy red hair and a lively intelligent face.

'I'll gladly answer any questions I can,' he replied in answer to Toye's preamble, 'but I honestly don't think I can add anything to what I told you last time.'

Pollard and Toye took him over the ground again.

'This farm machinery you saw in the field,' Pollard said, 'what sort was it?'

'I took it for one of those small tractors with a glassed-in cabin. You know – high up in front. But there was a tarpaulin chucked over it, and I honestly didn't look very carefully. You see, I'm a new boy in the practice,' he added with a grin, 'and I was hell bent on getting to Manor Farm before the cow passed out.'

'We gather that mother and child are doing well,' Pollard said. He asked a few more questions, and then deciding that nothing was to be gained by prolonging the interview, he departed with Toye after thanking Mr Howlett for seeing them so promptly.

When they were in the car Toye looked at him interrogatively.

'Fairlynch yet again,' he replied. 'You know, there's something that doesn't fit in in all this but I can't put my finger on it. Perhaps being on the spot will dredge it up from my subconscious.'

As they drove once more through Spireford Toye commented on the dustbins and bags of rubbish outside the cottage doors.

'Some villages only get a collection once a month I'm told,' he said. 'Unhygienic, I call it.'

They drew up at the white gate leading to Mill Cottage. Just inside were two dustbins, and a pile of stout cardboard containers of the type used by wholesalers for dispatching groceries to their retailing outlets. Pollard suddenly sat bolt upright.

'Do you see what I see?' he demanded. 'High up in front, Howlett said. Half a dozen of these stacked on the roof of Rossiter's car over the front seat and that tarpaulin chucked over them...'

'Reckon you're spot on,' Toye said with the gruffness of genuine admiration.

Pollard was aware of ideas flooding

through his mind.

'Of course it's all wrong,' he said excitedly. 'I've got there at last. This is a water meadow.'

Toye invited him to come again.

'A water meadow's low-lying grassland by a river, with the water table – the saturation level – very near the surface. When the river's in flood the water seeps up and there are pools on the surface, and the river water often comes over the banks as well, bringing jolly useful fertilising mud. The standard drill is cutting for hay one year and grazing stock the next. Obviously it's grazing this year, so why a tractor?'

'Handy place for parking it?'

'That's what we're going to find out. Come on. Hayes at Manor Farm will know who farms this field.'

By a stroke of luck they encountered the farmer a short distance along the road. In response to a signal from Pollard he drew up in his Landrover, got out and came over to them looking wooden and suspicious.

'Who farms Mill Meadow?' he repeated in reply to Pollard's question. 'Why, I do. It's Fairlynch land and part of the farm. What's wrong with that?'

'Nothing, Mr Hayes. As it's a water

meadow and under grazing, I take it you aren't using a tractor there this year?'

Pollard got a surprised look.

'Know about water meadows, do you? Yes, that's right. I take a crop of hay off it alternate years, see? What's all this in aid of?'

'It's been reported to us that a farm vehicle looking like a tractor was parked there during the night of last Saturday week.'

Mr Hayes' eyes narrowed.

''Tweren't mine.'

'Might one of your neighbours have parked one there?'

'Naw. Doesn't make sense. Plenty of room at the next farm up the road for theirs, and nobody's going to come up along here from the far side o' Spireford. Someone up to no good, maybe?'

'Keep it under your hat, Mr Hayes, if you don't mind.'

With a curt nod the farmer returned to his Landrover and drove off in the direction of the village.

'None of this adds up to proof, you know,' Pollard said. 'All the same I think we've shot our bolt here for the moment. We'd better head for the Yard to see if Chilmark is pulling off anything. We'll just look in at the police station and let them know what we're doing.'

A message was handed to him asking him to ring Mr David Harrow at Fairlynch Manor when he came in.

David Harrow was once more apologetic.

'I hope I'm not being officious and tiresome,' he said. 'I thought perhaps I'd better pass on a call I've had from Mr Gilmore this morning. I rang the office yesterday afternoon as you suggested, and got on to a secretary who said she'd put another set of plans into the post at once: no problem at all. Then about ten o'clock this morning Mr Gilmore rang me himself and seemed a bit short, I thought. He asked if the first set had turned up as it wasn't convenient to let us have a spare. I said it hadn't, but that I'd send back the second one as soon as it did. Then he rang off pretty abruptly.'

'Thanks for letting me know about this,' Pollard said. 'I'd like you to keep me posted of any further developments. You can get me at this number and extension...'

He went out to report to Toye.

'If Gilmore's getting edgy, we may have found a weak spot,' he said. 'By the way, the stains on that folder were made by contact with mud and gravel identical with the samples you took outside the front door at Fairlynch.'

On the following morning there was still no message at the Yard from Professor Chilmark. Pollard brought his Assistant Commissioner up to date on the case. After the latter had underlined the point that most of the evidence was either unsupported or circumstantial or both, there was nothing for it but to retire to his own room and tackle the backlog of work on other cases. This was so extensive that when a call from Milan was put through to him at five o'clock he had to make a rapid mental realignment before taking it.

Professor Chilmark was commendably brief and circumspect.

'Chilmark here,' Pollard heard. 'Mission successfully accomplished. I hope to get the morning plane and be with you at your HQ in the early afternoon, bringing exhibit.'

'Right,' he replied with equal circumspection. 'We'll be expecting you.'

He leant back in his chair with a mounting sense of excitement, and after a few moments flicked the intercom switch on his desk.

'Get me Inspector Toye, will you?' he said.

When Toye appeared Pollard gestured towards a chair.

'Sit down and listen,' he said. 'A call's just come through from Chilmark. He's due back at lunchtime tomorrow with Great-uncle Gilmore's "Flight" in his suitcase. God only knows how he's done it. The AC is being snooty about unsupported evidence and whatever, and we've got to work out a proposition to put to him. I want to see if any of my ideas survive the cold water you always pour on 'em...'

They talked until late in the evening, resuming the conversation the next morning after Pollard had made a half-hearted attempt at dealing with his backlog. Their deliberations were cut short by the un-expected arrival of Professor Chilmark at midday, explaining that he had managed to transfer to another airline with an earlier flight. He gave the impression of decorous elation as he put a small travelling case on Pollard's desk and began to open it.

'Wonderful what a friend at court can do for you,' he remarked, taking out the Gil-more painting and propping it up with some books. He eyed it critically. 'Not a bad effort, is it? The old josser had a bit of talent. But the thing wouldn't fool anyone with even minimal specialised talent for more than a couple of minutes. The canvas is out of period to start with, and you'd get far more stretching in a genuine early-eighteenth-century painting... You've got a lab and some chaps lined up for proper testing, I expect?'

Pollard had, and after lunch the technicians took over. His presence was not required or even particularly welcomed, but he wandered into the laboratory during the afternoon and watched the proceedings for a time. He felt envious of the investigations' strictly limited field of enquiry and the unchallengeable character of their results. No unpredictable human factors here to reckon with.

The outcome of the tests, a fully attested if foregone conclusion, was available in time for a meeting with the Assistant Commissioner late in the evening. Professor Chilmark was invited to attend, and his account of his dealings with the cathedral authorities at Portrova, backed by the support of his highly-placed friend in the Ministry of Fine Arts, was extremely diverting. In addition to bringing back the substituted painting, he had also been able to get police confirmation of stays in North Italian hotels by Malcolm Gilmore and Hugo Rossiter over the critical period.

'You'd better join the CID,' the Assistant

Commissioner remarked. 'You seem to have a natural grasp of investigation. Will the Portrova people shut up as they're getting the Lecci back?'

'Undoubtedly,' Professor Chilmark assured him. 'With art thefts from churches running at their present level, they're counting themselves lucky.'

'Unfortunately,' the Assistant Commissioner said, turning to Pollard, 'our job's clearing up the homicide, not the art theft, and the available evidence is far less conclusive. What do you propose to do now, Pollard?'

'Stick to the original theme with your permission, sir.'

'Don't be so bloody cryptic. What do you mean?'

'A confrontation in the form of a further substitution, sir. Something along these lines...'

The only development of interest over the weekend was a call from David Harrow. He reported that during his absence at the committee meeting in London on Friday, a man had rung Fairlynch Manor saying that he was speaking for Gilmore Constructions, and asking if the missing set of plans and estimates for the tea room had been found.

Kit Peck had taken the call and replied that he did not know, but would pass on the message. There had been no further call.

'I don't see what Gilmore's getting at,' Toye said. 'Why's he het up about it?'

'I think he's quite unnecessarily jittery about that folder on two counts,' Pollard said thoughtfully. 'When Peck saw him off on the top terrace he – Peck – would have been holding the folder by our reckoning. He was well-known to be a careful bloke who'd put things away in their right place, particularly important papers connected with his job. What Gilmore thinks happened, I don't know. Then we questioned him pretty closely about dropping Peck after the party. He was quite explicit, saying they talked for a couple of minutes about the work his firm was doing, and then Peck got out and waved him off when he'd turned his car. Any suggestion that Peck went into the house and upstairs out of the way is the last thing he'd want us to cotton on to under the circumstances.'

'You've got something there,' Toye said meditatively.

By common consent they took Sunday off, Pollard taking Jane and the twins for another strenuous but satisfactory day on his brother's farm. Once again, after a snack supper and a look through the Sunday papers, he found himself getting up to switch on the television set for the late news. He had an odd sense of history repeating itself, and felt absurdly relieved that the usual reports of violence were all international in character.

Monday moved forward inexorably. He drove down to Wellchester with Toye in time for a lengthy conference with Superintendent Maynard and Inspector Rendell. Later he visited a local magistrate, returning with a warrant for the arrest of Hugo Rossiter on a charge of murdering Francis Peck, and another for the arrest of Malcolm Gilmore as an accessory to the crime. He had also obtained a search warrant for Mill Cottage and its outbuildings.

'Rossiter will plead guilty to manslaughter and get the murder charge dropped, wouldn't you expect?' Toye asked.

'Pretty well a certainty, I should think. He obviously never meant to kill Peck... What price we can't shock an admission out of either Rossiter or Gilmore tomorrow?'

Toye was reassuring. At the hotel they met Professor Chilmark who had just arrived. Pollard found himself welcoming the prospect of a third party's company for the rest

311

of the evening. Time passed, more swiftly and easily then he had anticipated. He woke on the following morning confident of holding a potentially winning hand. Everything would depend on how it was played.

Discreet observation had been kept on Hugo Rossiter and Malcolm Gilmore throughout the weekend. The latter had paid a lengthy visit to Mill Cottage on Sunday, but neither had shown any sign of leaving home. Except when away Hugo Rossiter was accustomed to spend Tuesdays at his art shop in Wellchester, and the invaluable Sergeant Bland had ascertained in conversation with his girlfriend that Malcolm Gilmore had no outside engagements on this Tuesday morning. By previous arrangement Toye called each of the two suspects soon after nine o'clock, Pollard meanwhile following the conversation on an extension. They were told that it had been decided that the five stolen pictures could now be returned to their owners. Superintendent Pollard would be at the police station to hand them over at ten-thirty. Malcolm Gilmore was asked to collect his 'Flight into Egypt' and his wife's 'Inspiration', and raised no difficulty, even sounding relieved, Pollard thought. Hugo Rossiter was told that his presence was necessary as an organiser of 'Pictures for Pleasure'. His sarcastic comments on red tape were met by Toye's courteous and unruffled reference to necessary formalities.

'Now they'll ring each other,' Pollard said as he put down the receiver. 'I hope to God Maynard's chaps have got them trailed all right, that's all.' He went off for a final check of his preparations.

After what seemed like an interminable wait it was ten twenty-five. Watching from a window with Toye, Pollard saw Malcolm Gilmore drive into the car park with Hugo Rossiter in the passenger seat. The two men sat in conversation for a couple of minutes before getting out.

'Right, then,' he said tersely. 'Over the top.'

Toye went towards the main entrance of the police station, and engaged in conversation with the duty sergeant. Pollard slipped into a room next to the one they were using as an office. He listened to Gilmore and Rossiter being escorted there by Toye.

'If you'd kindly step in here, gentlemen,' Toye was saying, impeccably correct, 'I'll fetch Mr Gilmore's two pictures. Superintendent Pollard will be here in a few moments with the necessary forms for signature.'

Malcolm Gilmore responded with a remarkably raw comment about waste of time. Toye emerged, raising his eyebrows as he took the paintings from Pollard, and returned to the next room to hand them over. He came out again, and rejoined Pollard outside the door which he had left just ajar. They listened tensely.

There was a brief exchange of comments followed by an explosive exclamation from Hugo Rossiter.

'Christ! They've rumbled it!'

'What the hell do you mean?' Malcolm Gilmore's voice cracked in staccato incredulity.

'It's not the Lecci, I tell you. It must be yours.'

'You know bloody well it can't possibly be mine. If it's not the Lecci, it's yours, that what it is! So that's been your dirty game – substituting your copy for the Lecci. I see it all now, why you were so keen all along, you bastard. You're not getting away with it, though. Either you hand over the Lecci when we're out of here or I'll turn Queen's Evidence. At least I'm not a bloody murderer...'

A crash and a shout brought Pollard and Toye into the room which suddenly filled with police. Blood was running down Malcolm Gilmore's face, and a painting in a broken frame lay on the floor. Toye and a constable quietly stationed themselves behind Hugo Rossiter.

'Why don't you arrest him?' Malcolm Gilmore snarled. 'Can't you see he's assaulted me?' He tried to staunch the flow of blood with his handkerchief.

In complete silence Pollard picked up the 'Flight into Egypt'.

'Ask Professor Chilmark to come in, please,' he said to a constable at the door.

He watched Hugo Rossiter carry out a swift mental calculation, and Malcolm Gilmore became suddenly immobilised, blood-stained handkerchief in hand.

'Good morning, Professor,' he said calmly as the small but impressive figure walked into the room. 'Would you be kind enough to look at this painting and tell me if you recognise it?'

Professor Chilmark took the 'Flight of Egypt' from him and scrutinised it carefully.

'I am prepared to state on oath,' he replied, 'that this is a painting which I brought back to England last Friday with the permission of the cathedral authorities of Portrova in North Italy. It is a late-nineteenth-century copy of an original work by the Venetian artist Lecci painted in the early-eighteenth-century, for which it had been substituted.'

'We know the actual date of the substitution,' Pollard said almost conversationally. 'It was June the seventeenth 1977, and was accompanied by an assault on an English woman tourist who happened to be in the cathedral at the time–Yes, officer?'

A Wellchester sergeant handed him an oil painting identical in size with the one held by Professor Chilmark.

'Acting on your instructions, sir, and with a warrant, we searched the studio of Mr Hugo Rossiter at Mill Cottage, Spireford, and found this picture hidden in a cupboard.'

'Thank you, Sergeant,' Pollard said. 'We now have a further link in this complicated chain of events. This second copy of Lecci's "Flight into Egypt" was prepared to be…'

'I know nothing whatever of this nonsensical business,' Malcolm Gilmore burst out. 'I don't possess the technical skill to carry out an art forgery. If there was a substitution…'

'There was a witness to the substitution,' Pollard replied. 'Ask Mrs Julian Strode to come in, please.'

Pale but composed, Julian Strode walked in. She wore a sleeveless silk frock, and a cardigan was draped over her shoulders. She carried a scarf and a handbag. Malcolm Gilmore made an involuntary backward movement.

'Mrs Strode,' Pollard said, 'when you were attacked and tied up in Portrova cathedral in June 1977, was one man involved, or two?'

'Two,' she replied unhesitatingly.

'That won't stand up in court,' Malcolm Gilmore shouted. 'She couldn't possibly have seen with her cardigan over her head!'

There was an electrified silence, broken by a short laugh from Hugo Rossiter.

'Kaput!' he remarked sardonically, and saluted Pollard.

The publishers hope that this book has given you enjoyable reading. Large Print Books are especially designed to be as easy to see and hold as possible. If you wish a complete list of our books please ask at your local library or write directly to:

Dales Large Print Books
Magna House, Long Preston,
Skipton, North Yorkshire.
BD23 4ND